Desperately
Devoted

A Novel
K. C. NiBlack

ISBN 978-0-615-24882-0

Cover design and artwork by K. C. NiBlack

K.C.Niblack@gmail.com

Sites of Interest:
http://www.myspace.com/niblackenterprises

Desperately Devoted

Lord, if I had ten thousand tongues, I still couldn't praise you enough...Thank you!

K. C. NiBlack

Acknowledgments

Before anything, I give thanks and honor to God. He gave me the vision, the drive, the ambition, and the testimony. Thank you.

Mama, you molded me and raised me to be a woman of integrity. Thank you for instilling the values in me that you have. It may not have seemed like it then, but you are appreciated. I love you. Daddy, I miss you and I love you. Thank you for being such a great example of what a real man, and father is. To my brothers, Kevin, Keith, Korey, and Kolby...I love you guys, and I have always believed in you. My daughters, you inspire me, and make me want to push harder. You two are the best daughters a mother could ask for. I could not have been blessed more with such well-behaved, loving, sweet, creative, smart, and just plain great girls as you two are. Mommy loves you so much. Remember to always do it right the first time. My aunts, thank you for checking in on me from time to time. It really means a lot to me. To my niece and nephews: Jordan, Brianna, Davis, and Jackson, I love you so very much. I wouldn't trade you for the world. To the special people that God has placed in my life: Angel S.-I miss our coffee gatherings in the mornings. You always had a smile for me; April E.-I'll never forget sitting in the driveway at three a.m.—you know what I'm talking about; Bianca B.-what can I say? There's just so much...from learning about what the lonely do on Christmas, to the ever beloved "Coyote Stories." I can't depend on you if I was locked in a closet, but I know you'd be there for a "Symphony Run"—you know what I'm talking about... and you know that's why I love you (lol). Callie R.-my bestest childhood friend, you were there from the beginning—when I found out what drama really was (i.e. youth camp meeting). From the "you don't love me, you don't care about me, you don't want to be with me forever and ever!" to the "come and get'cho prize!" I still watch "The Five Heartbeats" and think of you! I love you so much. Charnika H.-you truly inspired me...thank you. Ebony S.-I'm sure your shoulder is worn out from me, but thank you for always lending it for me to cry on. Jeannette J.-my soul sista! I love you girl, and can't wait to see you again...yes you can! (lol).

Desperately Devoted

Kieona J.-my baby sis, you keep me laughing, boo. I miss our "spoken word" moments at the millennium...only us (lol). Lisa P.- thanks for checking in on me, and for your prayers. You're a great person—don't ever doubt that. Nina & Tater-I love you guys so very much, you are definitely family. Otescia J.-thank you for all your love, support, encouragement and inspiration. Staci P.-my big sis...girl! Where do I start? We have been through too much...only things that sisters could really share. I love you. Stefanie B.-my sister, I am so glad God saw fit to keep us together...thank you for everything. My friend and fellow author, Stephen Earley Jordan II, thank you for the guidance throughout this process, you're great. Tanesha C.-we always felt like we were looking in a mirror...your prayers, and words of encouragement really made things easier. Thank you; Tanishia D.-you are true to your word, and I appreciate that. You have proclaimed yourself to be one of my biggest fans, and I have to say, I can definitely count on you to cheer me on. Thank you. I love you; My dear friend, Terry Newsome, thank you for always speaking the truth to me, and allowing God to use you through your awesome voice—which changes lives. I am so glad to have you in my corner, thank you. Wanny R.- I love you so much girl. You are the epitome of strength, whether you believe it or not. You are real, you are unique, and you are my sister. I thank God for allowing our paths to cross. To all my supporters and readers, I appreciate you far more than words can say. Thank you. Oh, and I can't forget the haters. God bless you...keep doing your job. As long as you're hatin' on me, I know I'm on the right track.

If I failed to mention your name, charge it to my head—not my heart.

One

FRANKIE LEONE STOOD in the lobby of the leasing office for the twenty-three story, condominium building located near the Nation's Capital overlooking the Potomac River. The lobby's ceiling was close to twenty-three feet high itself. There were a set of traditional style columns that introduced the waiting area which was festooned with a burnt orange colored rug, mahogany wood end tables, velvet midnight blue chairs and luxurious golden brown linen curtains which were suspended from the cathedral-style window. Frankie looked around as she stepped onto the brown ceramic tiled floor that preceded the waiting area. This building complex was known for offering some of the most luxurious studio apartments, and condos in Fairfax County. The complex offered many amenities such as a fitness center with state of the art equipment, an indoor Olympic-sized pool as well as an outdoor one for the summer months, and a sauna—all of which Frankie desired. A business center was also on-site that included computers, high-speed internet, copiers, and fax machines. There was a rooftop club for tenants to entertain guests or to relax, and simply enjoy the view of the city. Each unit came equipped with stainless steel appliances, granite countertops, washers and dryers, and built-in XM Radios that came equipped with surround sound speakers housed throughout. The complex was one block from the subway—which was also a highly sought after commodity by many of the locals. Being able to catch the subway, as opposed to driving a car, and sitting in traffic, would definitely save her time and money—both of which she could use more of.

This location was perfect for Frankie being that she had just landed a senior accounting position with one of the most prominent financial accounting and consulting firms in the nation, Wallace NVest Financial Corporation—located in the heart of D.C. She had been researching this firm, along with many others during her senior year while she attended grad school at the University of Florida. After carefully comparing various firms, the benefits, perks, incentives, and potential for growth offered by Wallace NVest definitely made Wallace NVest stand out in front of the crowd. Frankie had her heart set on that position. For four years straight, Frankie sent them her resume along with letters of recommendations, and proof of various awards, and certifications that she had received. Wallace NVest was a reputable company, and it was known that it was difficult to land a job with them. Many believed that it all boiled down to who you knew that would determine if your application even got a second glance—regardless of how qualified you were. When they finally called for an interview, after four years of Frankie's persistence, she knew that she wouldn't need time to think about it or weigh any other options—the hefty sign on bonus was a plus too. After the interview, they offered her the position. She accepted it there on the spot. She knew from the beginning that Wallace NVest was where she wanted and needed to be. She had been working for a smaller financial firm in Florida, and just wasn't happy there. It paid the bills, but that was it.

She fumbled through her brown and pink Coach bag looking for her cell phone that had been ringing nonstop for the past fifteen minutes. She pulled out her white and pink floral zippered make-up bag, and held it up in the air with her left hand. Her thick, long black hair fell into her face as she lowered her head to look closely into the bag. Using her right hand, she brushed the hair out of her face, sweeping it behind her ear. Some often questioned Frankie's ethnicity. She was very fair skinned with shiny, thick, long black hair. Her face was slender and her cheekbones were high. She had long black eyelashes outlining her dark grey eyes that held the turbulence of a cloudy sky. Her thick full lips always shinned with clear gloss, and her radiant smile showed off perfectly straight, white teeth. Her legs were smooth and long—just like her arms, and were slender and toned—compliments to the many years of ballet lessons. She continued to dig through the rather large handbag with her right hand. She pulled out a half empty bottle of water that she had forgotten was still in there from that morning. She walked over to the large circular wastebasket, and tossed the bottle in the trash. The phone continued to pipe out the theme music to "Good Times" as she continued to rummage through the designer bag.

Frankie, still holding the make-up bag high in the air with her left hand, walked over to the velvet midnight blue chairs, pulling her Coach suitcase behind her. The glass coffee table in the middle of the waiting area was covered with various magazines. Frankie sat down in one of the chairs, and slammed her purse down on top of the magazine covered table. By the time she was able to locate the phone, she had completely emptied out her purse. Her lilac and vanilla lotion, Gucci sunglasses, pens, notebook, travel size deodorant, lime and coconut body spray, mints, eyeglass case, tissues, sewing kit, socks, iPod, book, Palm Pilot, fingernail file, gold thong sandals, wallet, mail, and her purple mini-accordion style file case—which contained all the documents she would need in order to secure a place to live, were now covering the layers of magazines.

Frankie looked at the phone as it lit up and began to play the theme music again. It was Reese Thorton, Frankie's best friend of thirteen years. Frankie pressed the green talk button with a French manicured thumb, and placed the phone up to her ear. Before she could speak, Reese was screaming on the other end so loud that Frankie had to move the phone away from her head.

"It's about time you answered your phone!" Reese shouted.

"I was on the subway heffa! Stop screaming in my ear. It is *too* early for that. Is everything okay?"

"Everything is fine. I was just sitting here…expecting a call from you." Instantly Frankie knew what the problem was as she took note of the exaggerated sadness in Reese's voice.

"Reese, girl I am so sorry." Frankie closed her eyes, and lowered her head. "I know I was supposed to call you as soon as I landed, but I was so anxious to get here to get everything taken care of with my place."

"Ummm-hmm." Reese responded. Frankie imagined that Reese was pouting with her arms folded. Frankie smiled as she began to pick up all her personal belongings, and place them back into her purse. As she was doing that, a tall, slender, white man with spiky blonde hair stepped out of a side office, and walked up to her. He was dressed in a light blue and white pinstriped summer suit with a white cotton dress shirt underneath that was unbuttoned midway. His eyes were blue and lined with black eye liner. His lips were shinning with a hint of rose tint to them. He stood before Frankie with his hands folded in front.

"Uhh…Reese, I have to let you go." Frankie said as she raised her hand to the gentleman. "Let me take care of this, and I will call you as soon as I'm done."

"Ummm-hmmm." Reese responded. Frankie closed the phone shut, and placed it back in her cargo space of a bag. Frankie carried that large purse whenever she had a day full of errands to run. Normally, she carried a very small handbag that would only hold her wallet, a compact mirror, and her cell phone. Frankie was all in all a neat freak, and couldn't tolerate clutter. She was also very prepared. She looked up at the man who was waiting patiently as she placed the last of the items back in her purse. Frankie stood up as he introduced himself.

"Guut morning…You must be Ms. Leone. I am Sebastian. Just Sebastian. I am zee manni-jure." He spoke with a French accent that was obviously rehearsed. Frankie tried not to laugh.

"Yes. I am Frankie Leone. Nice to meet you."

"Great! Now zat vee have zat out of zee vay…follow me." Sebastian twisted around, and began to walk back towards the office he had originally stepped out of. He led her to his office that was decorated beautifully. The walls were painted a sage color, and were lined with cream-colored crown molding. Directly across from the entrance of the office was a window that covered the span of the entire wall. There were gold-colored panel sheer curtains that flowed from the elegant cream-colored valance—which coordinated perfectly with the sage wall. A desk sat in front of the large window, and was adorned with various sized frames containing photos of a white Pomeranian pooch. To the right was a fireplace that had a contemporary oak and silver mantel. Above the mantel was a rather large mirror that climbed the length of that wall. To the left of the room was a row of oak and silver file cabinets that matched the fireplace mantel flawlessly.

Sebastian asked Frankie to take a seat in one of the dark leather wingback chairs that sat in front of the desk. Frankie sat down, placed her bag in the chair next to her, and crossed her legs. Sebastian walked behind the desk, and sat down as well. He turned on the computer screen that sat at the edge of his desk, and pulled out a handful of pamphlets from the middle drawer. He noticed Frankie looking at the photos of the dog on his desk.

"That's Lovely. My Pom. Isn't she to die for?" Sebastian placed his hand over his chest as he grabbed one of the many photos. He kissed the picture, and inhaled. He loved his dog. Frankie simply smiled as she grabbed the pamphlets that Sebastian had tossed her way as he took a moment to honor the pooch. "These are zee floor plans we have available. You are vellcomed to look at vich-ever von you like. Vee have zee von-bedroom an zee two-bedroom. Vee even have zee studio style. All of zem are gorgeous, no?" Frankie continued to nod her head as she studied the layouts.

"Do you have anything on the top floor?" Frankie asked as she began to read the specifics that were printed at the bottom of the page.

"I don't zink so…you would like for me to check zee database, no?" Without an answer from Frankie, Sebastian began to punch the buttons on the black keyboard. He mumbled to himself. "Ah…you are in luck darling. Vee do have zumthing for you. Come! Let's take a looksee, no?" Sebastian reached for a set of keys that were in a glass bowl on the other side of his desk. Frankie grabbed her purse, and followed him out of the office down a corridor that led to six elevators. They both stepped in, and waited patiently as the elevator ascended them to the twenty-third floor. The doors opened slowly, and Sebastian stepped out into the foyer. Frankie followed.

Desperately Devoted

Sebastian placed a key into the keyhole, and twisted the knob. He opened the door, and walked inside. Frankie followed closely. When she laid her eyes on the room, she fell in love. Instantly, she began to place her furniture, mentally. Sebastian was walking around flinging his arms in the air as he gave a very animated and charismatic tour of the penthouse. Frankie walked around, and examined the rooms. They were fairly large and spacious. The rooms smelt of fresh paint, and the carpet was obviously new. Frankie walked into the master bathroom, and stood in the entrance with her hand over her chest in awe. The bathroom contained a large garden tub that was positioned directly in front of a massive panel window that overlooked the city. She could see the Washington Monument from where she was standing. Frankie was sold. The asking price *was* a little more than she was expecting to pay but she could handle it. Frankie was not one to live above her means, however, if it meant that she could juggle things around, and cut corners in other areas financially, to get what she wanted then she would. Sebastian showed her some of the other community amenities as they returned to his office. She signed the paperwork, and placed the keys to her new home on her key ring. Satisfied with her decision, she walked outside and phoned Reese.

"Girl, you have *got* to see it! It's off the chain! My mouth hit the ground when I saw the bathroom." Frankie turned around, and looked at the building itself, and smiled. "I'm done now, so do you want me to meet you at the shop?"

"I'm almost done here too. I can come to you so that you can give me the grand tour. I'm glad you found exactly what you wanted. I was starting to think that you would never find it. You know how picky you are. All bougie 'n stuff." Reese teased. "We can go to dinner and celebrate too. And I'll show you around town...things have really changed since you were last here. There are also some people that I think you are going to flip out when you see." They both hung up after finalizing their plans to meet up. Frankie decided to venture out, and take a walk down the street lined with little cafés and boutiques as she waited for Reese to show up. Frankie pulled her sandals out of her bag so that she could switch them out with the red high-heels that she was currently wearing. Before pulling off her pantyhose, Frankie looked around to see if anyone would see her. The coast was clear. She pulled the pantyhose down and off. She rolled them up into a ball, and placed them inside her bag. With her feet now breathing a sigh of relief, and feeling the cool breeze of the wind on them, Frankie placed the heels in her purse. She slid the sandals on, and took off down the sidewalk—which was filled with people dressed in jogging suits, business suits, or casual wear. She blended into the crowd, and kept up with their upbeat pace. There were people on cell phones carrying on meaningless conversations and some were conducting business. Some were running trying to catch the next train that was pulling up at the station. Others were enjoying lunch at the cafés that were scattered along the sidewalk. Buses were flying past, along with people on bikes that sped by just as fast. This environment was definitely a drastic change from the slower pace of the Florida town that Frankie had become accustomed to. But she knew that this would be just what she needed…a change.

Two

REESE TIPTOED QUIETLY behind Frankie who was seated outside of the coffee shop reading a book. Reese placed her hands over Frankie's eyes.

"Guess who?" Reese whispered in her ear. Frankie turned to see her best friend standing there with an ear-to-ear grin spread across her face. Frankie jumped up, grabbed her friend, and hugged her tightly. It had been over a year since they had last seen each other when Reese had flown to Florida to visit Frankie last winter. Reese had wanted to get out of the harsh cold weather of Washington, D.C.

"Look at you Reese Cup! Your hair! You colored it!" Frankie patted auburn and brown highlighted curls that framed Reese's face. Reese and Frankie were like night and day. Frankie was fair skinned, and Reese's skin resembled that of creamy milk chocolate. Frankie was tall, and Reese was a few inches shorter. Frankie was a very conservative dresser, and Reese was over the top. Reese didn't have a problem showing her cleavage or her legs, and had tattoos and piercings in more places than just her ears. Frankie kept her earrings to a maximum of two—one in each ear, and she had only *toyed* with the idea of getting a tattoo, but never followed through with it. Frankie's mother had always wondered why Frankie still socialized with Reese. "She's too much trouble Frankie! You really need to cut her out of your life," her mother would say. "That girl is going to get you into a lot of trouble." Frankie always thought to herself that it was amazing how easy it was for someone on the outside looking in to judge without even getting to know the person.

Reese was the closest thing to a sister that Frankie had. She met Reese in the third grade. Frankie had just moved to Winter Park and was the new kid on the block at Clarkdale Elementary. She didn't have any friends, and it was hard for her to make them.

Frankie was sitting on a bench making designs in the dirt with her feet. Every now and then she would look up, and watch the other children play. In between making a heart with her left foot and watching a group of girls play hopscotch, Loretta Green, the biggest third grader in their class, approached her. She and her two sidekicks, Ivy Thompson and Jackie Foster, walked up, and surrounded Frankie. Loretta wore her hair in two thick French braids that needed to be brushed. She was overweight and used it to her own advantage. All the children were afraid of Loretta. Loretta's mother seemed to be ten times Loretta's size—which intimidated the teachers.

Frankie slid back on the bench trying to distance herself from Loretta. Loretta started making fun of Frankie's hair, her clothes, her shoes—anything she could think of, she was ragging on it. Ivy and Jackie were pretty much there to simply co-sign, and encourage Loretta. Ivy and Jackie were much smaller than Loretta. Ivy was a darker toned, scrawny girl who always wore braids in her hair. Jackie was light skinned with sandy brown, kinky hair that she wore in a huge ponytail on the side of her head. The three girls always wore overalls and matching shirts underneath. This day, they were wearing white shirts covered in yellow and pink flowers.

Frankie stood up, and tried to get away but Loretta placed both of her ashy hands on Frankie's shoulders, forcing her back down on the bench. Frankie looked around. There were no teachers in sight. Frankie noticed that all the children had started paying more attention to what was going on. Frankie noticed a few of them pointing with fearful looks on their faces, and whispering to each other. Frankie also spotted a girl standing off by a huge tree with her arms crossed. They girl wore a pensive look on her face. The bullies continued to taunt Frankie, and laugh at her expense until they were interrupted by a voice.

"Leave her alone wit'cho big self Loretta! You always messin' wit somebody!" Loretta, her sidekicks, and Frankie turned to see the girl that was leaned up against the tree now standing there in her torn jeans and t-shirt.

Loretta laughed at her presence as if the girl was a waste of time to even worry about. "Reese, you shut-up wit'cho dumb self. That's why you ain't got no daddy!" Pain flashed quickly across Reese's face but faded just as quickly. Reese lowered her head, and walked away with her hands in her pockets. Frankie felt horrible for her because she figured that this girl didn't know her from Adam, and she was willing to stand up to this Amazon monster on her behalf. Frankie turned her attention back to Loretta, anticipating what would happen next.

Loretta and her crew began to laugh harder, louder, and crack more jokes as Reese disappeared behind the huge tree. Then they turned *their* attention back to Frankie who was now biting her bottom lip, nervously. Frankie glanced around frantically in hopes that she could spot a teacher to get some help. All the children were just standing there with fear in *their* eyes as well.

The next sound Frankie heard was a loud crack.

CRACK! Loretta's face turned from hateful enjoyment to extreme pain in a matter of seconds. She instantly fell to the ground. Then there was another crack.

CRACK! And then Jackie fell to the ground holding her head.

CRACK! Then Ivy. And by the time Ivy hit the ground, the three of them were screaming in unison. Frankie saw a pool of blood beginning to form around her feet. She looked up in horror, and standing there with a two-by-four in her puny hands, was Reese with *the* most satisfied look on her face. It was almost creepy. Reese threw the board down and stood over Loretta, now smiling.

In a cold and calm voice Reese said, "Now I told you to leave her alone wit'cho big self." Reese stretched out her hand towards Frankie. "Come on. Get up fo' you get blood on your shoes."

Frankie grabbed her hand and hopped over the three wailing girls. Reese proceeded to lead Frankie away from the pile of bullies. Then she stopped in her tracks as if she had forgotten something, and hollered back. "And no, I ain't mad that I ain't got no daddy. He dead, cause I shot him!" Reese yanked Frankie's hand, and continued to walk off the schoolyard. "Well I'm going to get detention for this, but I can't *stand* Loretta." She looked at Frankie. "Don't nobody ever say nothing to her!"

By this time, the teachers were running towards Frankie and Reese screaming. They grabbed both girls, and off to the principal's office they went. The girls sat in the hallway while they waited for Principal Cumberland to come out of a meeting. Frankie knew that she wouldn't get into too much trouble when her parents found out what exactly happened. But she would definitely hear from her mother that she needed to make sure she didn't keep Reese as a friend. She would see Reese as bad news. She also knew that her mother would consider moving her to a private school. From that moment in the schoolyard, Frankie and Reese were thick as thieves. Although they were like night and day, they couldn't seem to be apart from each other. Reese was always getting into trouble, and Frankie was constantly trying to stay out of it. Reese was always ready to fight, and Frankie was the peacemaker. Reese had a rough childhood, and Frankie's was stable with two parents. Reese had three older brothers. Frankie was the only child. Reese taught Frankie a lot about the streets, and Frankie tutored Reese in history. Reese allowed Frankie to see that prejudging someone based on the first impression was sometimes the best thing to do. She would constantly tell Frankie to believe someone when they showed who they really were. "When someone shows you their true colors, believe them," she would say.

When it came to Reese, what you saw is what you got. However, she also learned through her relationship with Reese that no matter how rough and tough someone was, they were still human and they cried just like the next person. Reese was a great person and only allowed a hand full of people to get close enough to know that. Frankie felt blessed to be one of those few. As different as they were, at the end of the day, they never let anything come in between them. They became like sisters. If you saw Reese, you saw Frankie. All Frankie's school events, Reese was there, rooting her on. All Frankie's quizzes, it was Reese who was the one testing her. All the late night tears, it was Reese who was the one wiping them away. But now, as adults, there *were* certain things that Frankie had to distance herself from because she had an image to uphold—but would do anything for her, still to this day and Reese knew it.

"Yeah, I colored it." Reese said as she patted her own head. "Wanted to try something new." Reese reached over a grabbed a handful of Frankie's dark locks. "When are you going to let me do something with all this?"

"Girl, you know I ain't changing anything with my hair. I can't do like you, and try all those different colors and shades. I would look crazy." Frankie explained.

"Now you know I would *not* have my sister walking 'round here looking a hot mess." Reese studied Frankie's hair. "Just think about it…I'll hook you up girl. Anyways…ready to roll?" Reese clasped her hands together and smiled at Frankie. They walked out of the coffee shop arm in arm like they used to do when they were girls.

Three

FRANKIE FOLLOWED REESE into the restaurant. Jordan's was the latest hotspot, and was particularly crowded on Friday evenings. It was extremely loud. There were waitresses darting in and out of the crowd with trays full of drinks and entrees. The sound of plates and glass clinking together rang through the air. Each table was dimly lit by a mini emerald green lamp—which was suspended from the ceiling. Couples were leaned into each other peering into each other's eyes, probably whispering phrases that they had heard from previous relationships. Groups were huddled in various booths laughing loud and enjoying their meals. Several familiar faces were scattered throughout the bar and were having an obviously good time. Frankie tried to put names with the familiar faces but couldn't.

Reese walked up to the podium and told the young girl her name. The young girl waved for Reese to follow her. Reese turned to Frankie and grabbed her hand. Frankie was still looking around the restaurant racking her brain trying to figure out if she knew some of the people she had just seen. She followed Reese and the teenage girl through the maze of tables and booths. They turned the corner, and stopped at the end of a long table that sat over twenty people. Frankie looked up to see a table full of old high school friends that she hadn't seen since their all night grad party, eight years ago. Everyone smiled and got up to greet Frankie. She heard a variety of comments as everyone hugged her. Reese went to go mingle with those that had already welcomed Frankie.

"Hey girl, you haven't changed a bit!"

"Wow, Frankie! You look good girl!"

"It is so great to see you after all these years."

"Where the hell have *you* been all these years?" Frankie was so delighted to see all their faces. She couldn't wipe the large smile off her face. As she reached for an empty chair, someone else grabbed it. She looked up to see a face that she thought she would never see again. Her heart stopped. It was Anthony Davis—her first love, and her high school and middle school sweetheart. They had dated since the seventh grade. Everyone thought that they made a cute couple—everyone except her parents. Actually, it was her mother that was adamantly against Frankie developing a relationship with Anthony. Anthony was not raised in a wealthy, upscale home. He was raised in the Southeast District of D.C— not the most ritzy or luxurious suburban area. Bottom line, he lived in the ghetto and Frankie was raised in the uppity "white folks" part of town. Because of the county line divisions, all the children, regardless of class went to the same school—unless they were enrolled in Hillcrest Academy, an influential and especially expensive private school. Frankie had begged her parents to allow her to go to public school and they, to Frankie's surprise, agreed to it. Not only did Anthony live in a different world than Frankie, a single mother of five—which Frankie's mother believed was never a good sign, raised him. She felt that any boy who did not have a father in the home was destined for failure and a life of crime. Anthony was not ashamed of where he came from. He was proud to have such a strong mother, and knew that he would grow to be a better man than his father ever was—whoever *he* was.

Despite the criticism from her mother, her aunts, and other Bourgeois family members, Frankie couldn't help the fact that she loved him. She tried to force herself to not love him, but she soon realized that the one thing she could not control was her heart.

At a point in Frankie and Anthony's relationship, Frankie's mother forbade her to ever speak to Anthony again. Frankie was then forced to sneak around. She couldn't breathe when she wasn't around Anthony. She was truly in love with him. And he was with her. She knew that Anthony was not destined for a life of crime. She felt in her heart that he would prove her mother wrong. As time went by and they got older, Frankie began to indulge in benefits of her chic and lavish lifestyle. The only problem with that was that Anthony couldn't afford to give her those things. He spent a good bit of his free time working a part-time security job at the mall to help his mother out as best he could. This irritated Frankie. Not only was she being condemned for dating a guy who was less fortunate and influential than she was, now she would have to face judgment for dating a security guard.

Frankie tried to accept his lifestyle. She turned her head the other way when she felt it was beneficial to her. She had become so influenced by her mother's view of life, and so engulfed with the idea of marrying wealth that she soon became a woman that Anthony didn't recognize anymore. He felt as though she was trying to mold him into something that he knew he would never be—fake. When Frankie would bring up college, Anthony would dismiss the idea. Anthony didn't want to go to some four-year college to earn a degree in something he had no passion for. He was content in attending the Police Academy, and working hard for something in which he *did* have a passion for—justice. He felt that he wasn't college material, and he knew that he didn't want to work a nine-to-five behind someone's desk. Anthony knew in his heart that he wanted to be a police officer working the streets—the same streets that he grew up on. The same streets he witnessed his older brother, Marcus, being gunned down by a dirty cop over marijuana. The streets that he saw innocent girls being deceived into selling their bodies to get all those lavish items that Frankie took for granted. When he explained his dream and his passion for law enforcement to Frankie, she blew it off—figuring that it was a phase, and that he would eventually come around. She *knew* that she would not be able to allow him to do *that*. She loved Anthony, but she was beginning to love her image even more. Frankie contemplated breaking things off with him several times because she had always imagined her life to be similar to that of her mother's, her aunts, and cousins. They were all married to rich men, and lived posh lifestyles where they hardly ever lifted a finger except to go shopping, or to get their hair and nails done. Frankie pictured herself being married to a successful lawyer, doctor, or stockbroker—never a cop.

She thought about the very first time that she saw Anthony. He was standing off in the back corner of the cafeteria with his friends. They were always having a good time laughing and joking during the lunch break. The teachers all loved Anthony, and always felt that he was really going to do great things with his future. So whenever Anthony and his friends would get a little loud in the cafeteria, the teachers never really said anything. They figured that there were worse things that they guys could be doing. They were harmless.

Frankie was walking with Reese from the cafeteria line to her table, with her tray in her hands. She heard the guys laughing, as usual, and glanced in their direction. The guys were having a really good time. Between them getting loud and rowdy, and the general chatter of everyone in the room, the noise level was quite high. Frankie and Anthony's eyes connected. And for both of them, at that moment, it felt as though the room fell completely silent. They both felt as though they were the only ones in the room. Their connection lasted for only a few more seconds before they were brought back to reality. Throughout the rest of the lunch break, they shared periodic glances, mixed with smiles, as they both tried to stay engaged in the conversations that were going on around them.

After school one day, Anthony spotted a long-legged Frankie walking towards a black Lincoln town car. Frankie was wearing a pink cashmere sweater, and a brown and pink pleated tennis skirt. Her brown and pink plaid socks were pulled up to her knees. She was wearing a pair of white sneakers that were obviously brand new. Her hair was scooped up into a thick black bun, and she wore a pink and brown ribbon around it. Gold designer earrings hung from her earlobes—which swung back and forth as she pranced along. She was placing a pair of designer sunglasses over her eyes when Anthony reached her. He tapped her on the shoulder, and smiled generously when she turned around to face him. Anthony was taller than she was, and his eyes were deep and dark, like the night. His teeth were like pearls and his smile could tame a thousand beasts. His skin was smooth and dark brown, like cocoa. Not a flaw in sight. His hair was jet black and he kept it cut low. Thick, smooth eyebrows fit his face perfectly, complementing his full, soft lips. Anthony had broad shoulders and muscular arms, accurately proportioned to his legs. He was visibly in shape.

Frankie's heart jumped when she turned to face the cutie from the cafeteria. She lowered her shades and peered over the rim at him with a slight grin building on her face.

"Yes? Can I help you?" She asked with poise.

"Hi. You don't know me…"

"You're Tony Davis. Sure, I know you. Class clown." Anthony was honored that she knew his name.

"Well…I was wondering if…you would be able to…uhh…" Anthony stumbled over his words. Before he could gather the courage to invite her out on a group date to the movies, the back passenger side door window of the black car slid down. The voice of Frankie's disapproving mother sounded off.

"Frankie? We have an appointment dear."

"Yes ma'am." Frankie responded agitated, desperately wanting to hear what Anthony had to say. She opened the car door and climbed inside. Anthony stood there blissfully as he watched the love of his life drive off. Anthony was persistent, and made it a point to show Frankie how interested he was in her. One day, Anthony approached Frankie during school hours where her mother was nowhere around and was finally able to ask her to join him and a group of friends to the movies. From that point on, they became a pair and love began to build. Anthony stood on that curb watching Frankie, at the tender age of thirteen, drive off not realizing, of course, that he would be standing just like that five years later watching the love of his life drive off, again heartbroken and hurt as opposed to the high he was on at that moment. Frankie would finally tell him that he wasn't enough for her and that she was leaving to attend college in Florida, and that she was sorry that things had to end that way.

Anthony stood there, now as a grown man, peering into Frankie's eyes, still holding onto the chair. An outburst of laughter from Reese as she clowned around with a group of guys at the other end of the table awoke Frankie from her reverie. She was speechless. A lump formed in her throat and she didn't realize that her mouth was slightly opened. Anthony reached up and lifted her jaw shut.

"Ole' Key Lime…you're still as beautiful as the day I saw you in the cafeteria." He said amiably while positioning the chair so that she could sit down in it. He bent down and kissed her on the cheek. Frankie's face was hot. She felt like it was on fire. Her heart was racing, and it felt like it was going to burst out of her chest any minute now. *I can't breathe!*

"Tony…hi." Frankie responded ruefully. She didn't know whether to run and hide her face, or just stand there. She wondered if he had ever forgiven her. She sat down in the chair as her mind began to race. She then began wondering if he was still single. Did he have any children? Was he happy? What had he been doing these past eight years? Did he hate her? Frankie couldn't think straight. Anthony's presence had completely thrown her off.

Four

AFTER DINNER, FRANKIE'S whole demeanor had changed. She rested her right cheek on her hand, and peered out the window of Reese's car door, as Reese sped through town. Reese noticed that something was troubling Frankie. She reached down from the steering wheel, and popped Frankie on the left thigh. Frankie mumbled without looking up.

"Huh?"

"What's the deal girl? You've been acting funny ever since we left Jordan's. You okay?" Reese glanced back and forth between her best friend and the highway.

"I'm fine." Frankie lied.

"Key…I know you better than that. Fess up."

"Dang girl…I was fine. I was doing great until…Tony showed up. I didn't know he was going to be there." Frankie sighed deeply, and continued to look out the window.

"Girl please…it's been like what? Fifty years…"

"You know what I mean, Reese." Frankie shot Reese an aggravated look, and then turned her head to look back out the window.

She was feeling guilty all over again. Frankie had learned over the course of the previous eight years that money didn't equal happiness. Frankie wanted what she had with Anthony, and was having a hell of a time trying to find it. "I felt horrible all over again when I saw him. I bet he hates me."

"Yeah right, Key. That boy ain't worried 'bout you. That was eons ago. Let it go! I'm sure he did. Hell, you think he would've greeted you the way he did if he *hated* you? You're such a drama queen, sis." Frankie was too disheartened to snap back at Reese. Reese was right anyway. "You wanna grab some movies?"

"Nah girl...just take me to June's house. I just want to go to bed." June was Frankie's cousin. He was an illustrious attorney with his own firm in the heart of D.C. June was more like a brother to Frankie. They had grown up together, and acted like siblings. She normally would have made plans to stay at Reese's place, but it had been a while since she had spent some time with June, and she knew that he rarely had time to get away from his office. She also knew that she would see more of Reese than the law should allow. Reese's face perked up when Frankie mentioned June's name. Reese was interested in June, but he would never give her the time of day. Frankie noticed Reese's reaction. "Whatever, Reese. June ain't studdin' you either." Frankie giggled, and Reese sucked her teeth.

Reese pulled up in front of the iron gate—which surrounded the high-end community that June lived in. A guard walked up to the car and asked where they were going. Frankie called out from the passenger side.

"We are here to see June Matthews. I'm his cousin, Frankie Leone." The guard stepped back into the small kiosk, and picked up a phone. Moments later, the gates swung open, and Reese proceeded to cruise through them. The streets were lined with cookie-cutter houses.

The only difference between them was the color of the paint on the outside, and the coordinating shutters. The yards were all manicured identically, and just about every yard had a sprinkler going. There were a few residents walking up and down the sidewalks with their overly spoiled dogs sporting diamond studded leashes. Reese continued to drive at a snail's pace until she reached June's home. She pulled up into the driveway. They both saw June standing in the yard in his bathrobe and pajamas. He had a pair of leather slippers on his feet, and was walking the green garbage can to the curb. June wore a bald head. He was just as fair skinned as Frankie, and they favored each other quite a bit. June was slender and rather tall. He had very sharp facial features. High cheek bones, a pointy nose, small chin and hazel eyes. He had his Blue Tooth in his right ear, and was apparently on another call. By the time Reese pulled into the driveway, and put the car into park, June was finishing up his call. Frankie opened the door, and June smiled. Reese popped the trunk.

"Hey, Tweety!" he exclaimed walking briskly towards her.

"Bug!" Frankie replied. June grabbed his cousin, and hugged her tightly. Tweety was the nickname that the family had given her because she was so "yellow" and Bug…just fit. Reese had climbed out of the driver's side, and was standing there watching them embrace each other. June noticed her standing there, and greeted her as well.

"Hey there, Reese. Been a long time girl. Good to see you." He waved. Reese waved, and smiled. June walked to the back of Reese's car, and pulled Frankie's suitcase from the trunk. He closed the trunk, and placed the suitcase on the ground.

"Frankie…I'll see you tomorrow. I'll be at your place first thing to help with all the boxes. Have a good night, June." Reese blew Frankie a kiss, and climbed back into her car. As she disappeared down the street,

Frankie and June strolled up the driveway, and into June's home. Frankie walked over to the red plush sectional that was placed in front of a brick fireplace with a plasma screen panel television mounted to the wall over it. The television was turned to the ESPN channel, of course. June was a die-hard sports fanatic and Redskins fan. Frankie threw herself onto the couch and closed her eyes. She could hear the sounds of running water, and looked over to her left. She noticed, mounted on the wall, a decorative fountain. The sound of the lightly splashing water was so serene, and brought a sense of tranquility to the room. Before she knew it, she was fast asleep.

June had disappeared into the back guest room to prepare it for Frankie. When he came back out into the living room, he noticed his cousin nestled in the corner of the couch. Placing a gentle hand on her shoulder, he woke her from her sleep. Frankie stretched, yawned, and stood up. She wobbled, with her shoes in hand, behind June to the guest bedroom. There was a large king sized bed in the center of the room. It was adorned with tons of pillows that were various shades of blue and grey. The comforter was blue and grey, and was made of a combination of velour and silk. The windows were dressed in sheer light blue curtains with grey velvet valances. There was an oak chest that sat at the foot of the bed. Frankie's suitcase was on top of it. As Frankie began to search through her suitcase for her pajamas, June was in the guest bathroom turning on the shower for her. He came back out of the bathroom and placed a large, soft white towel, and washcloth on the bed.

"Your favorite soap is in there on the counter." June said as he pointed to the bathroom. Frankie, with sleepy eyes, thanked her cousin and shuffled to the bathroom with her nightgown, towel and washcloth in her arms. She closed the door behind her and began to undress. She stepped into the steamy shower, and could think of nothing or no one but Anthony.

Five

FRANKIE WALKED AROUND the empty penthouse as she waited for Reese, and the movers to show up. She was anxious to get settled in and get things in order. She knew exactly where she wanted to place her furniture, rugs, and where she would hang her artwork. Her favorite piece of art was an abstract painting that she had stumbled across at an auction one weekend. She had only decided to go to the auction because she had heard so many people talking about the great deals they had come across themselves. She went, not really expecting to find anything, and when the painting was placed on stage, Frankie's eyes became as wide as half dollars. The painting contained various tones of red, gold, brown, green, and orange. It was quite large, but it was beautiful. It would match perfectly with her brand new peanut-butter-colored leather living room set that she had recently purchased at Ni'Vecks Home Interior Designs and Furnishings. This store *was* pricey. However, everything that they carried was worth the price tag. The quality of their products was supreme, *and* their items were unique. They were so unique that one could be most certain that they would not walk into someone else's house, and see the same exact furniture in *their* living room.

Frankie had watched as the auction workers propped the artwork up on an easel in the middle of the stage. Frankie had observed the facial expressions of the crowd—to see if there was anyone else as interested in the mural as she was. The bidding started at five dollars and Frankie raised her hand. She ended up in a slightly diminutive bidding war with an older lady who eventually gave up when the bid hit six hundred and fifty-seven dollars. Frankie strutted proudly out of the warehouse, painting in hand and headed straight home to mount it on the bare wall that constantly screamed for attention in her living room. Frankie looked around the new place with her hand rested on her chin as she decided where she would hang it this time.

The buzz from the intercom broke the dead silence—which was almost deafening. Frankie jumped, and walked over to the small black box that was mounted by the front door. She pressed the white button that was in the right corner of the box.

"Yes?" She spoke into the box uncertainly.

"Miz Leone? You have zee movers here. I send them up, no?" It was Sebastian. Frankie snickered to herself.

"Yes Sebastian, you can send them up. I have been waiting for them."

"Sure. And zer is deese lady here who tells me she is vit you?"

"Does she have wild looking hair and kinda scares you?"

"Why, yes." Sebastian whispered into the phone.

"Yes, her name is Reese Thorton. She is with me. Send her up as well."

"Ohh-kay…vill do my love." Moments later, Reese was walking through the front door ranting, and raving about Sebastian downstairs. She absolutely hated being given the third degree, and apparently Sebastian had done just that. Frankie was sure it was because of how Reese *appeared* to everyone. But nevertheless, Frankie loved her.

There was a knock at the door—interrupting Reese's tantrum. Frankie laughed at Reese as she walked to the front door. She opened it. There stood a chubby man dressed in a pair of dingy blue coveralls. He had a slightly protruding belly, wore a pair of black steel-toe boots, and a fitted cap was on his head, pulled down over his eyes. His hands were large, his fingers were fat, and his knuckles were ashy. Frankie took note of his knuckles as she observed him scribbling something on the clipboard that he held in his hands. He lifted his head, and looked at Frankie. Instantly, they recognized each other. They both stood there in awe at the sight of one another.

"Eric Hamilton." Frankie said as she placed her hands on her hips. Eric took off his hat, as a grin began to form at the corner of his mouth— making his already plump cheeks look even bigger.

"Frankie Leone. Wow," was all he could muster up to say. It had been years since their last encounter. At the looks of him, she was glad that she had gotten him out of her system. He had really let himself go. She thought back to the time when she had really been addicted to him. She was weak for that man…years ago. While she stood there looking into his eyes, he tried to think of more to say at such an awkward moment. She reminisced briefly about her last night with Eric. She had just been stood up on Valentine's Day by some inconsiderate jerk. She had been on so many blind dates, and was flat out frustrated. After driving home with tears in her eyes, she had planned to just take a long bath and go to bed. It had been months since she had last heard from or saw Eric. So when her phone rang, and it was Eric, she had been taken completely off guard. She had pulled the phone out of her purse, looked at the display screen that read: "ERIC CALLING" and thought to herself, "Eric? What the hell is he calling for after all these months?" The phone rang a few more times as Frankie contemplated on answering the call. She knew that the minute she heard his voice, all her morals would be out the door. It was something about Eric that caused Frankie to lose all her dignity and self-respect.

"Hello." Frankie answered finally before it went to voicemail. Trying to sound sexy in between the tears she had just cried.

"Hey stranger…with your sexy self." The words rolled off his tongue so effortlessly. Frankie began to melt. Eric was like a drug to her. He was the smoothest talking, player she knew. And the sad thing about it was that she *knew* he was a player, and *knew* that he wanted only one thing from her. Every time she tried to resist him, the attraction would grow stronger. She began to throb between her legs, and if she could have slapped herself she would have. She threw herself on the couch, and while crossing her legs she placed a pillow from the couch in between them— trying to control the sensation.

"Stranger? You're the one who has been M.I.A for the past six months." Frankie had tried to not let her arousal show through her voice. She knew that the minute he got wind of it, he would be in her bed, and she was really trying to completely cut him off, and get her life in order. But his swagger, his voice, his physique just made her so weak.

"Well, you know my situation…what you doing tonight on this lover's night? I miss you." Eric began to slide his sneakers on. He knew that he could count on Frankie to give him one. Whenever he needed a really good release, he knew that all he had to do was call Frankie, and she would be waiting with open arms, and legs for that matter.

"Yeah…I know your situation, E. Why in the hell are you calling me anyways? It's Valentine's Day. Aren't you going to spend it with *her*?" Frankie tried to build up enough energy to tell him that he couldn't come over. She knew that he was planning on it. She figured that he was probably halfway to her house by now because he knew that she was weak for him. She figured that if she said the right things out loud, eventually she would piss herself off, and then she wouldn't want him at all. She felt stupid thinking that way, but it was what she was hoping would really happen. It never seemed to work. Her mind would just go back to the great sex that she would have with him. And that's all that they had—great sex. She didn't love him—well at least she didn't *think* she did. She didn't want to spend forever with him, because she knew the type of man that he was, and she knew that she would be his wife sitting at home while he was making plans to sleep with someone else—just as he was doing his girlfriend now. But there was always that small inkling of hope that *she* would be the one to make Eric want to settle down and be a one-woman man with her.

"Awe Kiekie...don't be like that baby. Let's not talk about her. I wanna talk about me and you. I miss your touch, girl. You be on my mind all the time." Eric was walking out the front door. He put his phone on mute as he turned his car on. He didn't want her to know that he was actually *that* confident in her inability to resist him—he didn't want to risk officially pissing her off, and never getting to touch her again. Being able to get her to bow down like she did whenever he would call always did something for his ego.

Frankie tried to snap at him, "If I was on your mind as much as you say, then why the hell haven't you called in six months, E?" She tried to keep her voice at a certain level. She also didn't want to completely piss him off because then he wouldn't come over. And oh how she wanted to be with him again. *Pull yourself together Frankie!* She didn't want him to come, and then again, she did. Eric always had her mind running in circles.

"Frankie, now I told you my situation. You wanna hook up or what? I'm feenin' you boo." He begged in the sexist tone that made Frankie fall to pieces. *Frankie! No...all he's going to do is come over, use your body and leave. He's not even going to spend the night and you know it! Say no, Frankie! Just say...*

"Okay...I'm home. Come when you're ready." *Idiot! You damn idiot! Now watch, soon as you are done allowing him to use you, he's going to get up, and go home to her! And you are going to go through that same pity party that you throw for yourself every time! You are so stupid! Stupid! Stupid! Stupid!*

"I'm on my way." Eric gave himself a pat on the back, and looked at his own reflection in his rear view mirror. He licked his finger, and rubbed his eyebrow. "You're a smooth mutha—shut yo' mouth!"

Eric stopped by the corner store to pick up a pack of condoms and a can of whipped cream. *We ain't played with whipped cream in a while...she's bout due.* The cashier, a young teenage boy with pimples all over his face, looked up at Eric, and snickered. He looked at the condoms that read: MAGNUM X-LARGE, and the looked at Eric as if he was a celebrity. Eric just winked, and continued on to Frankie's place.

Eric twisted the handle of the door, and as he expected, it was unlocked. He walked in, and heard soft music playing. Fragrant candles that were scattered throughout dimly illuminated the living room. He stood in the middle of the living room, and stared out the widow, taking a moment to enjoy the view of the lake that shimmered in her back yard. He saw Frankie standing on the patio in her lavender silk robe. She turned, and smiled at him. She was beating herself up inside, and wished that she had had more self-control. He walked over to her as he tossed the brown paper bag on the couch. He placed his hands on her neck, and rubbed his hands through her hair. Bringing his hand half way up the back of her head, he pulled her head back forcefully as he pushed her up against the stucco wall while kissing her neck roughly. Frankie's robe fell open, and Eric's hands began to roam all over her exposed body. He picked Frankie up, and she wrapped her legs around his waist. He turned around, and laid her down on the cement. The only thing between Frankie's bare back and the hard, cold cement was her silk robe. Thunder rolled in the skies as Frankie asked the Lord to forgive her because she knew that she was dead wrong, but it felt so good.

Rain began to pour as Eric continued to explore her body with his hands and his mouth. He ran his hands across her chest, and he kissed her navel. He gripped her thighs as if he was holding on for dear life, and kissed each one. He placed her French-manicured toes in his mouth as he used his hands to continue making her squirm in pleasure. He loved this power that he had over her.

He lowered himself down as if he were doing push-ups until his chest was pressing onto hers. He kissed her on the lips. He then reached down, and patted her on her thigh. She knew that meant that she needed to wrap her legs around him again. She obeyed. She wrapped her arms around his soaking wet body, and he picked her up again. This time he carried her into the living room out of the rain. Both of them drenching wet, they continued to kiss each other forcefully. He continued to pull on the back of her hair, and race his tongue up and down her neck. He reached down, and grabbed the brown paper bag while still wrestling his tongue with hers. Frankie leaned her head down, and began to kiss him on the ear. She knew that this was his weak point. She felt that she needed to gain some type of control, and not allow him to rule the night completely. He stopped dead in his tracks—losing focus for a mere second. She continued with a smile on her face. Whispering in his ear, and him responding made her want him even more. He carried her back to the bedroom, and continued where he left off on the patio. Throwing her wet body on the plush bed, he began to make love to her navel while massaging her chest. He sat back up, and at that moment Frankie reached for the edge of his shirt.

She reached down, and pulled his soaking wet shirt up and off his head—revealing his damp, dark chocolate rock hard chest. She threw the shirt over in the corner by the door. She then lay there rubbing her hands across his chest. She had loved touching his chest, and the ripples on his stomach. His body had been like that of a god. He was chiseled in all the right spots, and his skin was so smooth and soft. As she began to massage his perfect torso, he froze momentarily so that she could do so. He was so vain, and knew that Frankie loved his body. He watched her as she ran her fingers lightly over his stomach, and then down to his belt buckle. She pulled one end out, and then tugged on the belt to completely remove it. She unbuttoned the pants and tugged on them as well. He stood up and pulled his jeans down. He grabbed them, and threw them over with his wet shirt in the corner. He slid his shoes and socks off, kicking them over there as well. He pulled the little black plastic wrapper out, and began to place the condom on, all the while looking at her as he licked his lips. Frankie squirmed in anticipation. Her body was begging for him at that point, and her mind was constantly telling her to stop, and make him go home. *There's still time you nutcase! You don't need him! You are going to regret this in about one hour, and you know it!*

Eric lowered his chest to hers, and entered. Frankie's mouth opened as her eyes rolled in the back of her head. She moaned. Her eyes filled with so many tears that they began to run down the sides of her face. Eric kissed them too. While he continued to kiss her, he reached his left arm down, and grabbed the whipped cream. He sprayed it all over her, and licked up every drop. He then sprayed her neck and chest and continued to cover her and lick it up in a synchronized manner. While still moving as if they were dancing, he grabbed her right leg, and moved even faster. He patted her thigh again. She obeyed the signal. He picked her up, and forced her body to do what he wanted it to, and she allowed it. They began to move in sync, and faster. They fell up against the wall, and continued their escapade.

By the time they were both satisfied, they had completely destroyed her house. The furniture had been moved, the blankets from the bed were in the hallway, the table cloth was on the floor of the kitchen, pots and pans that were on the counter were strewn all over the kitchen tile. Eric and Frankie lay there on the floor of the laundry room panting and sweating. No matter how many times they did it, they always managed to find new ways that never got old. Frankie looked over at him, and began to feel regret. She had done it again. She had allowed herself to be used by him, and beat herself up for not having enough self-control or restraint to just say no to him.

Eric stood up, and began to gather his things. Frankie watched his naked body as he strolled into the bedroom. She closed her eyes, and shook her head while placing a sweaty palm up to her forehead. *Idiot! I told you!*

Within a few minutes, Eric showed back up with his clothes on, and her bathrobe in his arms. He tossed it over her naked body.

"Aye...I'm bout to roll." He said nonchalantly as he pulled his keys out of his back pocket. Frankie sat up, and pulled the robe on. She stood up, and tied the robe around her waist. Feeling as though she was standing completely naked in the middle of a room full of people, she pulled the robe tighter—up around her breasts. She glared at Eric, wishing

41

that this had never happened. He turned, and walked towards the door. She opened it for him so that he could walk out. He turned, and kissed her on the neck. He then began to lick again. Frankie placed her hand on his chest, and pushed him back.

"Bye, E." He winked at her, threw up the peace sign, and walked down the hall to the elevator to go home to his woman. Frankie closed the door, and placed her back up against it. She looked around her home, and couldn't believe that they had done that much damage. She didn't feel like cleaning up any of it, but she did anyway. She hated anything out of place. When she had finished mopping the kitchen floor, and her house was back to normal, she walked slowly to the bathroom to run some bath water.

While the water was running, she placed her hands around the edge of the sink, and stared at herself. She looked into her own eyes, trying to figure out why she allowed Eric, and all the others to mistreat her, and use her like that. Tears began to form as she just stood there, staring at herself. One crept out, and then before she knew it, she was balling. The water, splashing into the garden tub, created a sound that always caused Frankie to zone out. She began to think of a time when she would have never allowed this to happen to her.

When the tub was completely full, she turned the dial to lower the lights, turned on the speakers—which began to pump out sensual sounds of saxophones, and acoustic guitars. She removed the silk robe slowly, and lowered herself into the steaming hot water. She stared out the large window that provided the most serene view of the lake and the woods behind her house. That view was what had caused her to buy the house. Whenever the days got a little stressful for her, she would always run her bath water, and watch the moon flicker off the lake. As she watched the moon's reflection dance across the water, she would image herself on a beach listening to the waves crashing and watching the sunset. She pictured herself truly happy, and wondered what it would actually feel like. She wondered when the day would come when she would not feel any bitterness, any regret, any pain or hurt. With those thoughts floating through her mind, she closed her eyes and dozed off.

The sound of the elevator doors opening brought Frankie back to reality. Smiling and feeling like she had just won the lottery and trying not to laugh out loud as she looked Eric up and down, she asked, "So…how'd you end up here?"

"I…uhh…I work for Four Brother's Moving Company…they sent us the order…and…here we are…" Looking embarrassed, and feeling as though *he* was now standing naked, in a room full of people, he continued, "Frankie…you look really good." Frankie smiled, and began to discuss with him where she would like all her furniture to be placed.

Six

STANDING THERE IN FRONT of the massively large glass building that scraped the sky, brought an onslaught of butterflies to Frankie's stomach again. With her briefcase in one hand, she placed her free hand on her stomach, and took a deep breath. This day had finally come, and she wanted to take a minute to regain her composure, and get her nerves under control. Others rushed by her quickly, and disappeared through the revolving doors that stood before her. Everyone looked so rushed and busy. Frankie placed one foot in front of the other, and merged with the crowd. She was feeling rather confident in her grey and pink pinstriped suit. However, she was still nervous about her first day. This company was so large and so powerful, and she was tense about making a great impression.

The foyer of the building was large, spacious, and immaculate. In the middle of the room was a large glass desk. The glass was the color of jade, and there were mahogany wood accents on various parts of the furniture. Off to either side of the foyer were sitting areas that others were

44

taking advantage of. There were a few sitting and enjoying a latte while reading the newspaper. There were some pecking away on their laptops. And then there were others simply conversing with each other. People were in line waiting to sign in, ask questions, or request new badges that Frankie noticed hung around the necks of those who already had theirs.

There were three security guards that stood behind the desk assisting everyone that was in line. Two were men and one was a woman. They were all dressed in black uniforms. One of the men was a short, stumpy black man with only a bit of hair on the sides, just above his ears. He wore a pair of bi-focal glasses, and a gold-capped front tooth—which made itself noticeable every time he spoke. The other guard was a much younger brown-haired white man. He wore a diamond stud in his left ear, and kept a clean cut goat-tee. His eyes were brown and he was much taller that his fellow coworker. The woman looked to be in her thirties and wore a short cut. Her hair was excessively shiny, she wore a lot of make-up, and her eyebrows were painted on. Her orange nails were extremely long with designs, and rhinestones all over them, apparently to match the orange streak of hair that swooped over her right eye. Her fingers were covered in rings, and her wrists were engulfed in silver bangle bracelets. Her perfume was as loud as the popping sound she was making with her gum.

A lady in a black suit talking loudly on her cell phone about her weekend plans was in front of Frankie. Periodically, she glanced over her shoulder and smiled. Frankie responded with a smirk.

Frankie walked briskly to the elevators after signing in and receiving a temporary badge. The doors opened, she stepped in, pressed the tenth floor button, and rested against the back wall as other people began to fill the small space. As the doors began to close, a woman shouted out for someone to hold the doors for her. The woman turned the corner and stepped in just in time. Instantly, the woman's eyes grew to the size of golf balls when she saw Frankie. Frankie was checking the time on her watch and didn't notice the woman gawking at her.

"Frankie Leone." She said in an astonished tone. Frankie glanced up quickly. The doors behind the woman shut. "Oh…my…God! It is you!" The woman stepped in closer to Frankie, and at that moment, Frankie's mouth opened.

"Patrice! Oh…my…God! Patrice! How are you?" Frankie screamed. The two friends that had been separated for the past eight years acted as if there was no one else on the elevator. The elevator ascended to the next couple of floors as Frankie and Patrice hugged, cried, and hugged some more.

"You work here? You visiting? You interviewing? You auditing us? What are you doing here, girl?" Patrice was trying to gain control of her emotions but was having a difficult time. They both were.

"Yes, I work here now…in Acquisitions and Procurement. Tenth floor. You?" Frankie was smiling very hard, and so was Patrice. Others in the elevator were enjoying the reunion, and smiled as well.

"Shut the hell up! Me too! Girl!" This was all too unreal. But it was so perfect. With all the butterflies that were taking over Frankie's stomach, they were completely gone now. It had been close to eight years since Frankie had seen Patrice. They both had lost contact when Frankie moved to Florida. Frankie was the only one of Patrice's friends that had stayed in her corner after Patrice became pregnant in high school. Patrice became an outcast, and no one wanted to socialize with her any longer. It didn't bother Frankie that Patrice was pregnant, and Frankie never understood why everyone would have abandoned her the way they did. Frankie had been there from the beginning. She was there when Patrice found out that she was pregnant with Kayla, her oldest daughter. It was the summer before they started ninth grade. Reese's mother, Ms. Robin, was the cool mom. She was the one that they all trusted, and felt that they could talk to about anything. Ms. Robin bought a pregnancy test, and Patrice came over to take it. When she got the results, she cried like a baby. She knew that she wasn't going to get the support from her own mother who was constantly in the streets living her own life. Patrice's father was never around, and her mother was so strung out on cocaine, and so deep in the streets that Patrice was left to take care of her younger brothers and sisters. There was the baby sister, Jackie, who was only three at the time. Then there was Olivia, the five-year-old. Next came Joshua, he was nine. And lastly, there was her twin brother Freddie who, of course, was fourteen. Freddie spent a lot of time in the streets hustling so that he could bring food into the house. Patrice didn't want that kind of life for her brother, but they really didn't have a choice at that time in their lives.

Patrice was a good girl in high school. She was just vulnerable and naïve, and had become a victim of loneliness which disguised itself as love. Patrice had thought she was so in love with Wesley Tate, the athlete, when in actuality she just wanted someone to love her. Wesley took advantage of an opportunity to "get some" from a virgin, and played the game that he needed to play in order to get her to give it up. Patrice lost her virginity to Wesley, and not long after that, he broke up with her, and began to date Monica Jenson, a cheerleader in his grade. It wasn't long after the break-up that Patrice found out that she was pregnant. Wesley denied it and went off to college that same year. That was the last time Patrice saw or heard from him. Since then, Patrice had had two more children, Cierra and Kendra. Zion, a neo-soul musician with dreads, fathered them. She had fallen for Zion after she graduated from high school. He was an integral part of the girls' lives. He and Patrice weren't able to develop a well-rounded relationship due to the hectic schedule Zion's musical career came with, and his career wasn't as lucrative as he had wished. They were still cordial, and he loved all three girls as his own.

Patrice struggled but did everything in her power to make sure that she could provide a better home to her daughters. She worked a full time job during the day and went to school in the evenings so that she could earn a degree. It took her longer than it would have had she not been raising a family of course, but she stuck to it with the help of her twin brother, Freddie. Freddie watched the girls in the evenings while Patrice went to school. She was truly thankful. It had not been too long ago that she, too, had just started working at Wallace NVest and was feeling the same nervousness that Frankie was feeling.

They walked off the elevator, and Patrice immediately began to introduce her to everyone that passed them in the lobby. She introduced her to Amber, the receptionist, who didn't look a day over nineteen. She had long stringy blonde hair that looked wet. She wore a pink silk blouse and a black skirt. Her shoes were pink and black, and matched perfectly. She spoke very fast and in a high-pitched tone. Frankie just smiled and thought to herself *there is no way I am going to be able to hear that girl's voice all day!*

Frankie met so many different people that day that she couldn't remember anyone's name but Amber's. She received a complete tour, and orientation from Patrice and Amber, and ended up in a private office—her private office. The office was just right for Frankie—in fact, it was way more than she had expected. The company was obviously prepared, and waiting for her. Her name was already engraved on a gold plate and

48

posted outside the door of her office. The room was dark, and Frankie walked over to the window to open the blinds. She twisted the rod and stood there in awe of the amazing view of Washington, D.C. She turned around to take a better look at the office now that the sun was completely lightening the room.

A moderately large desk sat sideways in the office. It contained many cabinets and drawers. There was a bulky leather chair that sat behind the desk, and two smaller versions of it sat in front of the desk—for clients, she assumed. There was a beautiful Persian rug in the middle of the floor that contained dazzling hues of red, brown, and yellow—just what Frankie loved. A large plasma screen television was mounted on the wall directly across from the desk. A small row of file cabinets rested in the space beneath the television.

Frankie walked over to the desk, and sat down in the chair. She swiveled around in it. *I could surely get used to this!* She closed her eyes and thanked God. Her prayer was interrupted by a male voice.

"Looks like you found your new home. We've been waiting for you Ms. Leone." Frankie spun around to see a tall black man holding a coffee mug that read: #1 DAD across the front. He was dressed in a navy blue suit with matching dress shoes. His tie was covered in miniature saxophones and musical notes. He had thick black, slightly curly hair that was brushed towards the back as opposed to the front. He wore a thick mustache, and his lips were large. He smelt of coffee and pine mixed with some type of cologne that Frankie couldn't quite place. His skin was the color of caramel, and his eyes reminded Frankie of iced tea. They were very light brown and just looked…refreshing. He had a comforting smile that lit up the room even more than the sun did. He was a big man.

"Yes. This is lovely, sir. I am very pleased to be here. Like the tie." Frankie wasn't sure who he was so instead of making a fool out of herself, she opted to not say a name at all and hoped that she could break the ice by commenting on his tie.

"Well young lady, we were very impressed with your experience, your credentials, and your overall presentation. Welcome aboard. Oh, and the tie…well…when you have five kids, you can expect to get at least one good tie and a coffee mug every Father's Day." He laughed. He loved his kids. It was obvious. "My wife gets luckier than I do. She's gets the good stuff." He laughed again. He adored her. That was obvious too. "Well, I will let you get back to whatever you were doing. I just wanted to stick my head in and welcome you to the family." He waved and walked out, closing the door behind him.

Minutes later, Patrice walked in still wearing the smile that formed earlier that morning. "Hey Boo!" She giggled. Frankie just continued to smile. "So what you think about Mr. Wallace?" Patrice asked as she walked over to the desk and sat in one of the chairs.

"Mr. Wallace?" Frankie looked confused.

"Yeah…that was who you were just talking to, you nut!" Patrice giggled again and looked around the office. Frankie didn't know whether to be honored or go run and hide.

"*That* was *the* Mister—"

"Yep." Patrice kept smiling. "He flew all the way in to welcome you. He likes to make sure everyone feels at home. He's a great guy. You won't see much of him unless there's a problem that only he can fix. Other than that…we see him on the teleconferences." Frankie couldn't believe that she was actually *talking* to Mr. Wallace NVest himself! She shrugged her shoulders and prayed that she hadn't just made a complete idiot of herself.

Seven

IT DIDN'T TAKE FRANKIE long to catch on to the duties and responsibilities of her new job. Things came easy to her and before she knew it, she was performing very well. She had really fallen in love with her job. They were great people to work with and the company was just a great company to work for overall. She hadn't realized that she had been there over a year and was heading to her second.

The sound of the rain beating down on the skylight of her bedroom made it harder for Frankie to get out of bed. The rain always made her sleepy. Frankie turned over, and pulled the thick down comforter over her head. She was excited about going to the mandatory business conference that her job required them to attend once a year, but the warmth of her bed seemed more alluring. This conference was not only a great opportunity to meet new people and network, it was also a free trip with everything included. She couldn't complain, but at that moment, it *was* a tough choice.

Frankie groaned and turned over to look at the clock. Four-fifteen A.M.

What? I must have overslept! Frankie threw the comforter off and flung it to the left. She crawled out of bed and headed for the shower. The phone rang.

"I'm on my way!" Frankie screamed

It was Patrice. "Frankie, the plane is boarding in thirty minutes! You need to—"

"I'm on my way! Patrice, please call a cab for me! And call the front desk, and have the receptionist downstairs get the elevator ready for me in seven minutes!" Frankie slammed the phone down on the receiver, and showered as quickly as she could. She absolutely hated being late and having to rush.

She stepped out of the shower and began to dry off. She dried between her legs and noticed red on the towel. She cursed as loud as she could and ran to the other side of the bathroom to the vanity table. Leaning down with one hand on the table, she opened the cabinet door searching for her pads. She grabbed the bag and realized it was empty. She threw it down, and then searched for a tampon. *There has got to be one in here somewhere! Dammit!* She found a small box of tampons. She opened it up, and grabbed the last one that was in there. She unwrapped it and was just about to insert it when it slipped from her hands landing on the floor. Not only did it land on the floor, but it landed in the puddle of water that had formed from Frankie's drenched body.

Frankie was on the verge of tears by this point. She really had a low tolerance for high-stress. She took a breath, and figured that she was going to end up doing what she *had* to do, and absolutely *hated* to do. She ran, naked, through the living room into the kitchen and grabbed the roll of paper towels that read: NOW MORE ABSORBANT. She really hated to take it there, and she inhaled deeply as she ripped off about six sheets. She folded them longwise as she ran back to her bedroom.

She searched frantically through her dresser drawers for her tightest pair of panties. She wanted them as tight as possible so that the homemade pad wouldn't slip out as it had when she tried this same stunt in junior high school. *This is great Frankie! You're going to miss your flight right after you received that great evaluation from HR! Good goin' there kiddo!*

Frankie pulled the panties up her thighs, and placed the paper towels in the crotch. She then grabbed her pantyhose, and slid over to the bed to begin putting them on. She placed her right leg in and pulled the pantyhose. Then she placed her left foot in. As she attempted to pull again, her fingernail snagged it—causing a run to form. She cursed again, and decided to go with a pants suit.

Fumbling through her closet for her favorite black one, she pulled it out, and threw it on the bed. She looked around for a scarf to place around her neck. She found it laying on the edge of her armoire. She grabbed the pants, and pulled them up over her slightly damp thighs. She went to fasten them, and ended up having to suck in her stomach. She was bloated, and that suit never fit her right during that time of the month. She was running so late that she knew she was going to have to suck it up, and wear the tight pants. She put on the jacket, wrapped the scarf around her neck, and slipped on some sneakers. She had packed her pumps in the bag the night before. She grabbed her suitcase, purse, keys, and headed for the door. She had twenty-three minutes to make it to the airport.

She turned the corner to see Megan, the receptionist standing in the entrance of the elevator with her hand holding the side.

"Good morning Ms. Leone."

"Good morning, Megan. Thank you so very much. As you can see I'm very late. Is my cab outside?" The doors closed, and the elevator began to descend.

"Yes ma'am. Your cab is waiting. And you are welcome. It's no problem, especially for one of our favorites." Megan smiled as she watched the numbers light up.

"You guys are the best." Frankie complimented.

When the elevator doors opened, Frankie took off towards the exit doors. The taxi cab driver was waiting with the passenger side door and trunk already opened. She opened the lobby doors and shouted, "I'm sitting in the back and don't need the trunk! Thanks anyway! To the airport as fast as you can get me there!" She opened the backseat door, as she slammed the front one simultaneously. The driver ran around, slammed the trunk, and climbed in the driver's seat. Frankie threw her suit case in first and jumped in. They did it so perfectly as if they had rehearsed. "Let's go!"

"You got it!" The driver took off.

He made it there in ten minutes which was just enough time for Frankie to check in, and sprint to her gate. She gave him a fifty dollar tip, and climbed out of the cab as quickly as she could. She was relieved to see that the check-in line had no one standing in it, and the representative was very considerate of the fact that Frankie could possibly miss her flight. She printed out her tickets and pointed to Frankie's right.

"Gate 17!" the lady instructed. Frankie snatched the papers, and began to run down the corridor. She feared that security would cause her to miss her flight for sure. She placed her bags up on the metal table's conveyor belt, and walked through the security gate. She was pleasantly surprised that they didn't stop her this time. They usually did, especially when she was running late.

She made it to the gate, and saw the back of Patrice's head. They were still boarding. Patrice turned around apparently searching for Frankie. She grinned when she saw her, and rolled her eyes playfully.

Frankie walked briskly to the counter, and a woman scanned her boarding pass and pointed to the door. "Enjoy your flight ma'am."

"Thank you." Frankie joined the rest of the group boarding the plane, and stopped for a moment to catch her breath.

"Still ain't changed." Patrice teased. "You was always oversleeping. You almost missed graduation!" Laughing, they both boarded the plane.

Frankie placed her bag in the overhead compartment, and sat down in the leather seat next to Gary, a white guy in her group that rarely spoke. He had his iPod on and earphones in his ears. He looked up at Frankie, gave a small wave, and closed his eyes. Frankie sat down, and reclined her seat a little. She was thankful that she was able to relax in first-class seating, especially after the rowdy start she just had. It was only a two-hour flight, and she was determined to catch up on her sleeping. *Maybe I can continue my exotic rendezvous with that gorgeous islander, Juan...* She closed her eyes tight, and hoped that her dream would pick up where it left off.

Eight

THE PLANE LANDED and everyone's ears popped. Frankie stretched as she looked out the window. She watched as all the men in bright orange jackets raced to the bottom of the plane to grab the luggage. *At least it's not raining here.* Gary was sleeping with his mouth opened slightly and snoring. Frankie tapped him on the shoulder. He jumped, and looked at her. His eyes were red. The stewardess' voice came across the intercom to welcome them all to Orlando. The seatbelt indicator light chirped and turned off. Instantly, passengers began rummaging around for their bags and belongings. Frankie waited for her coworkers to make the first move. She looked back over at Gary. He was snoring again. Patrice had already gotten up and grabbed her things.

"C'mon girl…let's go so we can get our rooms. First ones there seem to get the better rooms." Patrice tapped Frankie on the shoulder as she walked past with her bags in hand. Frankie stood up and retrieved her bags from the overhead compartment as well. She leaned over and poked Gary on the shoulder one last time, and then proceeded to get off the plane.

Desperately Devoted

Patrice led the way walking quickly. Frankie did her best to keep up with her as she pulled her luggage behind her. The airport was magnificent. The hotel was located right inside the airport which Frankie found to be extremely convenient, and such a relief. She expected that she would have to chase Patrice all the way outside, and then rush to get into a cab. The lobby of the hotel was within the airport terminal. There was a large illuminated fountain that was surrounded by palm trees in the middle of the hotel lobby—which was, in fact, an indoor courtyard with skylights. Looking up, all the balconies that led to the hotel rooms could be seen. The front desk of the hotel was off to the right, past the fountain. Patrice had already made it to the counter, and was placing her room keycard into her back pocket. She stood off to the side as Frankie stepped up to the counter to sign in and retrieve her keycard as well.

As Frankie checked in, she spotted a very handsome, dark-skinned man sitting nearby on a bench by the fountain. He had his laptop out and was typing away. He looked up and connected eyes with Frankie. Trying to not even "go there", Frankie turned her head and attention to the young gentleman who was standing behind the counter in a red vest waiting patiently for Frankie to give him her information. She grabbed her keycard and turned to pick up her suitcase. The man glanced in her direction again, and Frankie simply smiled. He was bald and clean shaven. He was wearing a cream colored dress shirt with a chocolate brown tie. His chocolate brown slacks were slightly larger than his medium frame, and his matching jacket was laid over the edge of his chair. Patrice tugged on Frankie's arm to let her know that she was heading for her room. Frankie closed her eyes briefly, grabbed the handle to her suitcase, and began to follow Patrice to the elevators.

Because the hotel was so large, it took a few minutes for the elevator to reach lobby level. As Frankie and Patrice waited, a few of their coworkers filtered in, including Sharon Mills, their VP of Operations who was busy conducting business on her cell, and Mike Burzer, their immediate supervisor who was preoccupied in a what must have been very serious texting session. Sharon was a slightly heavy-set, middle aged black woman. She was quite short and could always be found sporting a classy designer suit with matching pumps. Sharon's hair was never out of place and her make-up was flawless. She was very sophisticated, highly professional and personable. Mike on the other hand was a tall, slender, very handsome, white man. His hair was dark brown and longer than the average business man's and his eyes were light blue. He always wore a black suit with the wildest looking ties. This day his tie was white and covered in palm trees. Mike was very hyper and made everyone nervous at times because he would just burst out the blue shouting for joy, or do something off the wall to "keep the party going" as he would say. Mike didn't bother Frankie. She found him hilarious, and his jokes always kept her laughing only because of how enthusiastic and proud of them he was, and how dry they were. Frankie just grinned. Before the elevator opened, Mike jumped up in the air and clapped his hands together very loudly. Everyone jumped—everyone except Frankie. Patrice looked extremely annoyed. Frankie continued to smile, however she was a little annoyed as well. Being that the sun had *just* come up.

"Okay guys! And gals! We got a long day ahead of us, but before we go to our first session this morning, I would love to have a quick huddle over breakfast. I'll meet you all back here in two hours." He glanced down at his Blackberry. "Yep! Two hours! Whooo! This is awesome!" Sharon continued with her conversation in the corner of the lobby. She had drifted off the moment Mike had leaped into the air. The elevator doors opened and a majority of them stepped onto the glass elevator. Those remaining waited in the lobby for the next set to come down.

As the elevator ascended and periodically stopped to let others step off onto their designated floors, Frankie turned to look out the glass walls, and onto the lobby below. She could see planes taking off in the distance. The elevator doors opened, and everyone dispersed in the direction of their suites. Before there was too much distance between them all, Mike turned and called out, "Two hours people! Act enthusiastic and you'll *be* enthusiastic!" Everyone mumbled and disappeared into their rooms. Frankie continued to walk down the hallway until she came to room 523. Patrice was fumbling with her key to room 525.

"I'll be over before we have to go down for breakfast with Mike's crazy ass…girl, he gets on my nerves…all loud…it's too early…" Patrice called out as Frankie's door beeped, and allowed her to enter.

"Okay. See you in a bit." Frankie walked into the room and was very pleased at what she saw. The room smelt of lavender and vanilla. There were chocolates in a small basket on the delicate silk covered bed along with a lavender colored Teri-cloth robe. She opened the sliding French doors that led to a balcony overlooking the airport runway and a bright blue sky. It was a wonderful view. Frankie stepped out, inhaled as deeply as she could, and looked up to the sky.

Not wanting to get caught up in the moment, and lose track of time, she quickly went back inside to unpack, and prepare for the breakfast meeting. She opened her bag, and realized that she did not pack her pumps as she thought she had. Frankie tilted her head back and tried not to scream. She hated to feel rushed. She never functioned right if she was being rushed. Walking out of her home earlier that morning, she had felt like she was leaving something. She sat on the edge of the plush king size bed and dialed the front desk.

"Hello Ms. Leone. What can I do for you?" The young lady asked. Frankie was impressed that they knew her name.

"Hello. Are there *any* boutiques nearby that I could possibly buy a pair of black pumps? Please tell me there is." Frankie pleaded.

The lady smiled. "Yes ma'am. Brianna's Boutique is right across the street. You may not have seen the sign, because they are renovating, and removed it temporarily. They don't open for another hour though."

"Oh bless you! Also, would you happen to know where I could purchase some…feminine items?"

"Gotcha…I can have room service deliver you some. They will be there within a matter of minutes. Let me know if it's not what you need, and I will take care of it." Frankie hung up the phone and looked around the room. It was decorated in a pallet of yellow, sage, and peach tones. Not that Frankie was particularly ecstatic over those color choices for her own dwelling, but she found this combination of colors quite tasteful. Frankie lay back onto the plush bed and gazed at the ceiling. There was a knock at the door and Frankie jumped slightly. She answered the door and on the floor was a small pink box with a yellow ribbon tied around it. Frankie picked up the box and carried it back into her room. She opened it up to find all sizes of tampons and a handful of pads. Frankie was *really* impressed.

An hour before she was supposed to meet with the rest of her group, Frankie left to go purchase a pair of shoes. There was *no* way that she would be able to show up in a suit and sneakers. On her way down to the lobby, she phoned Patrice to let her know where she would be. Frankie stepped out into the lobby and walked briskly towards the exit. The lady at the front desk waved and Frankie waved back.

"Power-walking in a suit? Wow, never seen that before." Frankie turned to see the man that was on his laptop, leaning up against the edge of the front counter. Frankie didn't have time to get smart with him, so she just smiled, and kept walking. She jogged across the busy street, and walked into the department store, scanning the area momentarily for the shoe department. She quickly spotted a pair of dress shoes that she knew would work perfectly. She put them on, placed her sneakers in the box, paid for them, pranced back across the street, her thick black hair bouncing behind her.

She looked over and saw Mike being seated in the café. He was steadily texting away. The man that Frankie connected eyes with was now seated back on the fountain bench typing away again. She glanced over at him as she walked back towards the elevators. He looked at her feet and smiled. Frankie grinned and disappeared behind the elevator doors to meet up with Patrice.

After breakfast, everyone proceeded to the conference hall which was immaculate and airy. The room looked as though it could fit over a thousand people and still have enough breathing room. There were people everywhere networking, passing out business cards, showing off pictures of their children and pets, and boasting about how great their businesses were doing. Frankie followed her co-workers to the registration table to grab name badges. As Mike led them all to their seats, Frankie looked up at the theater size audio-visual screen. The text read: 2008 NATIONAL FINANCIAL CONSULTATION ASSOCIATION GROUP ANNUAL CERTIFICATION: GUEST SPEAKER: DR. GREGORY B. TAYLOR, AAMS, CFP, CFS, CIMA, CIS, RIA, ChFC & CRPC. WELCOME.

Frankie was amazed to see that one person could carry as many designations as this Dr. Taylor did. Frankie thought to herself. *He's probably a prick.* As she took her seat, a slender, white woman who looked to be in her early forties, approached the podium that sat off to the left of the massive screen. She was dressed in a midnight blue silk suit with a rhinestone embellished collar. Patrice leaned over and commented in Frankie's ear. "Girlfriend is *wearin'* that suit!" Frankie nodded in agreement.

The lady then began to welcome everyone and introduce the speaker for the day. "Now please, give a warm welcome to Dr. Gregory B. Taylor." The crowd applauded and some stood to their feet. It was evident that he was highly esteemed. The man from the lobby took center stage. Frankie shifted positions in her seat and was so relieved that she hadn't taken the opportunity to cut him with her tongue in the lobby.

After a day filled with lectures and workshops, Frankie was exhausted. Patrice wanted to go sight-seeing with Gary, and everyone else drifted off to do their own thing. Amber and some others were headed to the pool. Frankie decided to join them. She put on her bathing suit and secured herself a lawn chair in the shade. She placed her shades over her eyes and put her ear phones in her ears. Closing her eyes, she listened to the smooth sounds of Ledisi. She felt someone sit next to her and assumed it was Amber.

Without opening her eyes, Frankie said, "That Dr. Taylor was very informative. Don't you think?"

"Yes, I must agree." The voice of a man caused Frankie to jump up. She lowered her shades to see Dr. Gregory B. Taylor sitting on the edge of a lawn chair. He was wearing a white cotton tank top that fit him like a glove, and a pair of green and blue, plaid, Nautica shorts. Frankie noticed that he had a tattoo on his upper arm that read: LILLIAN. She assumed that he was married, and then glanced down at his left hand.

There wasn't a ring nor was there a tan line. *It must be his mother's name, or maybe a sibling, or child.*

"Oh my goodness...how embarrassing...I do apologize...I thought you were..."

"It's okay. I find it flattering that you think I was informative." He smiled, and lay back on the chair. Frankie relaxed, and lay back down as well.

"Well you were...I enjoyed the lecture."

"Thanks...who are you listening to?" He asked pointing to his own ears.

"Ledisi." Frankie replied calmly.

"Love her. So smooth."

"Exactly." She agreed.

"So what brings you here this weekend?" He questioned.

"Here on business. My job." Frankie tried to not sound sarcastic, but failed.

Looking like he felt as though he had just asked the dumbest question in the world he said, "Well, yeah I figured that, but I guess my question should have been to ask what company do you work for?"

"Oh...I apologize. I work for Wallace NVest."

"Wow...what a great opportunity. That company is taking the financial industry by storm. And what I like about the CEO is that he's a real down to earth guy. He drips of integrity." He placed a pair of shades over his eyes, and crossed his legs at the ankle.

"Yes, you're right. I got the opportunity to meet him my very first day. He's a great guy." Frankie noticed Amber and some of her coworkers on the other side of the pool putting on sun tan lotion. Frankie wished that Amber had actually chosen to sit next to her so that she could possibly interrupt before she made a fool of herself with this gorgeous man.

Frankie and Gregory, for the next two hours, laughed, joked, compared notes about their personal likes and dislikes, and for the most part were having a great time. The sun began to set and their stomachs began to rumble. Frankie sat up and stretched her arms up above her head.

"I really enjoyed our conversation. I'm a little hungry, and tired. I think I'm going to go grab a bite to eat and call it a night." Frankie stood up and wrapped her towel around her waist.

"Have dinner with me tonight." Gregory invited as he fixed his eyes on her half naked body. He grabbed her hand, and then looked into her eyes.

"Well…I don't know about that. I don't usually date *married* men." Frankie smirked and picked up her iPod.

"What makes you think I'm married?" Gregory stood up, and grabbed his laptop case. Frankie pointed her index finger at his shoulder, over the tattoo as she sucked her teeth. "Oh, that?" Gregory smiled.

"Um-hmm." Frankie grinned with her lips turned up.

Chuckling, "That's my mother's name." He rubbed his arm.

Feeling silly, Frankie laughed it off, and then agreed to meet him for dinner. *It couldn't hurt. It's just dinner…even if he is lying.* They parted ways and planned to meet up a little later after getting dressed.

Frankie was ready to move on from her past and previously painful relationships. But she didn't want to get her hopes up and jump the gun. *It's just dinner Frankie. And you will NOT sleep with him!* She was trying to work more on her self-control and restraint. She wished that she could be a strong as Reese when it came to men. Frankie was constantly looking for someone to love her, and she had been giving herself away just to have a man on the receiving end making her *feel* like she was special. But that feeling only lasted for a short time, and then she felt like dirt again after it was over. She was hoping that one day she would find that special man who would be interested in loving her just for who she was. *Then* she would finally be happy. She knew that she had ruined her chances at a relationship with Anthony, so she would just have to settle for the next best thing. She also had to keep herself from jumping the gun, because it was as if any man that showed her the slightest bit of interest and affection, appeared to be "the one" in her eyes. And before she knew it, she was giving him her all—and all was her body.

After stepping out of the shower, she put on lotion, and slid her toe ring back on. She put on a cream colored linen suit and gold thong sandals. She tied her hair back into a classic bun, put on her gold and bamboo earrings, and went for the door. Before she reached the door, Reese called her on her cell phone.

"Hey girl." Frankie said as she turned the knob of her door.

"Hey hookah. How's it goin'?"

"Girl, you should *see* this hotel. We all got our own rooms; the service is high-quality. Everything is really nice."

"Yeah, I hear they be doin' it up. When will you be back?"

"Friday night."

"Cool…I'll bring some Chinese and movies over that night."

"Sounds good. I gotta let you go…bout to meet someone for dinner."

"Who? Patrice? Girl please, you ain't got to get off the phone with me cause you eating dinner with Patrice." Reese laughed.

"No…actually a doctor. His name is Gregory."

"Awwww sookie sookie now!" Reese teased.

"Girl please…it's just dinner. I'll see you when I get home." She closed the phone shut, and placed it back in her purse. By the time she got down to the lobby, Gregory was waiting for her by the fountain. She walked up to him, and they smiled at each other. He placed his hand on the small of her back.

"This way. You look stunning." He said as he walked her towards the steakhouse restaurant. The hostess sat them at a small table for two by the window that allowed them to view the airport runway. Their conversation picked up instantly as if they had never ended the conversation back at the pool. There were no dull or awkwardly quiet moments—which they both felt was a great thing.

"So where are you from, Doctor? Frankie teased as she took a sip of her wine.

"Please, call me Greg. I'm from D.C. actually, by way of New York."

"Really? I'm from D.C. too. What part of New York?"

"Brooklyn."

"Small world. Do you reside here in Orlando now?"

"No, I'm actually just here for the conference, like you. I live in Chocolate City. What about you?" He said as he took a sip of his wine as well.

"I just moved back to D.C. close to two years ago…from Atlanta."

"Small world for sure. You never know who may meet. Well we will definitely have to hook up again now that we know we are practically neighbors."

"Definitely." Frankie agreed with a smile. *If he was married, I would have picked up on it…I think.*

Nine

FRANKIE WAS SO HAPPY to finally be back home in her own place. She hated living out of a suitcase whether it was for a weekend or week— even if it *was* in a five-star, upscale hotel. There was just something about being home...in her own space...in her own bed. Frankie tidied up a bit and threw herself on the couch. Her front door flew open, and in burst Reese with her arms full of bags. She kicked off her shoes, shutting the door behind her with her right foot. Frankie turned her head towards her, and then turned her attention back to the television screen.

"You gon' help me heffa?" Reese yelled as she struggled with the bags. Frankie laughed as she jumped up to grab the food.

"Did you get my won-tons?" Frankie asked as she started snooping through the bags. Reese shot her an evil look. "Okay. I get it." Frankie threw her hands up and backed away giggling.

"So, how was your trip and dinner with the doctor?" Reese asked as she stepped into the kitchen to grab plates.

"Great. We have a lot in common." Frankie replied as she sat on the stool and watched Reese in the kitchen.

"Okay…that's all?" Reese walked back into the dining area and placed the plates on the table. She opened the container of rice, and handed Frankie the bag of won-tons.

"Well he's nice. He's got so many degrees and designations that it's unreal. He was the guest speaker. No kids. Never been married. Likes Ledisi…" Frankie began to scoop out the food onto the plates.

"Well…" Reese glanced at Frankie and smirked. "Sounds like a winner. Is he fine?" Reese grabbed her plate, the movie, and began to walk towards the living room. Frankie grabbed her food as well, and followed. Reese plopped down on the couch, and tossed the movie that she was carrying on the white bear rug. Frankie glared at her as she placed her plate down on the glass coffee table.

"Yes, girl." Frankie answered as she cracked open the movie case, and slid it into the DVD player. "He is fine."

"And he got money too?" Reese confirmed as she took a bite of her egg roll. "Yeah, sounds like a winner." Frankie joined her best friend on the couch and stuffed a won-ton in her mouth.

"Well, we shall see. I don't want to get my hopes up and get hurt again, but I really am ready to have someone in my life. I'm so tired of being alone or being in a relationship that constantly begins and ends in the bedroom. I want someone who is going to love me just because they love *me* and not the sex." She grabbed the remote and changed the channel.

"Trust me, I know the feeling all too well. Ever since that big blowout at the old barber shop with Shawn and his crazy ass wife…I still can't believe that I never saw the signs. I really loved him, and the thing about it was that he *knew* I loved him, and he *still* played with me." Reese turned her head towards the right wall and began to feel anger all over again as she mused over the painful experience. Frankie hopped up to go grab blankets from the linen closet as Reese's mind drifted back to that painful day.

Reese remembered it like it was yesterday. She was sitting in her own chair with her legs crossed, reading a magazine. Business was a little slow that day. The ceiling fan turned slowly, and the guys were huddled together in front of the television watching clips from the previous night's game. Reese looked over, and snickered to herself. *It's so amazing how simple they are.* When the clip cut to a commercial, the guys returned to their clients that were waiting patiently in their chairs.

"Man please! The Skins ain't going nowhere this next year! Mark my word!" Kyle shouted as he grabbed his clippers, and began edging his client up. Reese continued to read her magazine as a lady dressed in an extra tight dress walked in with a little boy holding onto her hand. She signed in, and sat down. The guys tried to continue their debate, but the lady with the painted-on dressed distracted them. Craig, the new guy, rushed to greet her and asked her what type of cut she wanted her son to get. She pointed at Shawn. Craig looked him up and down, sucked his teeth, and walked back to his chair.

The ladies that came through there always waited for Shawn. He was fine, and he was sexy. He had light green eyes and caramel colored skin. He wore a fro-hawk and was just...different. He was exotic and very intelligent as well. He was a definite head turner, and a keeper. Reese watched her do her best to catch Shawn's eye. Reese giggled to herself and continued to turn the pages.

"Man, look, yeah...the Skins messed up this year, but watch what I say. They are going to spank some serious rump next season." Shawn argued. He was D.C. born and raised, and was a loyal, die-hard fan. The guys always got a kick out of how serious he was about it. Reese loved to tease him as well.

"Shut the hell up, Shawn. You know the Patriots gon' run game on them like they did in that last game. They might as well just bend over now!" Reese added without even looking up from her magazine. Shawn glared at her. The lady with the hooker-like outfit on tightened her lips and shot Reese a jealous glance. The fact that Reese was the only woman in the barber shop made it easier for her to get up close and personal with Shawn which pissed a lot of women off. Even the ladies who worked in the sister branch of the barber shop, which was actually a beauty salon, were real nasty to her—well at least that's the way it seemed to Reese. Her response to their sideways glares and looks was always crude and vulgar. Reese steered clear of the beauty salon side just to cut down on the drama in her life. Shawn also begged her to stay away from them. Reese really loved him, and to keep him happy, she honored his request.

"You know what Reese, you make me"—Shawn put his clippers down and turned to her.

"Love you too, Chump!" Cutting him off, Reese closed the magazine, and turned to look at him. She winked, blew him a kiss, and he rolled his eyes. The lady in the painted-on dress eyeballed Reese. Because she was trying to be more professional, Reese didn't say anything to the lady. Although her tongue was ready to slice and dice her up one side and down the other. She may have been there just for eye-candy but little did she know that Reese was un-wrapping that candy on a regular basis. Reese smiled as she reminisced about their escapades that no one knew about. Like the one they had enjoyed the night before the huge blow-out.

Desperately Devoted

The customers had all been serviced and gone, and all the barbers and beauticians had closed out and left. The radio was still on, and an upbeat stepping song was playing. Reese began to sway her hips to the beat and sing along while counting the stack of money on the counter. She didn't realize that Shawn had come up behind her until he started dancing up on her back and singing along with the radio too.

Ain't no need to worry no
Everything is alright
Got my girl by my side
Everything is alright
As we step the night away
Our problems soon fade away
Got my girl by my side
And everything is
Alright
Alright

She continued to count the money with Shawn dancing behind her. She tried to stay focused, but whenever he came close to her she couldn't.

I'm gonna hold her close, yeah
Gonna move to the grove, yeah
Got my girl by my side, yeah
And everything is alright
Yeah, it's alright

Shawn pulled the money from her hands and turned her around. She tilted her head to the side and tightened her lips while folding her arms. "Shawn, I've gotta finish counting this money so we can get out of here." He kept singing with the radio and began to dance with her. He grabbed her hands, and led her to the middle of the shop as they started stepping together. Reese always let her guard down around Shawn because he had a certain hold over her. She loved him. She often fantasized about what their relationship would be like if they were able to finally tell everyone that they were seeing each other. She hated having to keep it quiet. Shawn's explanation was that if word got out that he was involved, his clientele would die down. Majority of his clients were the sons of horny women—who would give their left arm to be in Shawn's presence. He was just that addictive.

So in the meantime, she continued to play along so that others wouldn't be skeptical. She cussed him out in public, and he acted as if he couldn't stand her. They were great actors, and were fooling everyone. The only problem was that Reese was tired of playing the role. She had lately been pressuring Shawn to go public. She felt that there may have been more to the story that he was feeding her as to why they couldn't go public about their relationship...quite yet. She had even offered to go work at another shop. She was in the process of opening her own beauty shop anyway, and tried to convince him that his clients would never find out. He was adamant. She couldn't sway him. But because she loved him, she abided by his rules.

The song faded into a slow jam and they began to kiss passionately. Reese let him take her right there, behind the counter, in the middle of the barber shop. That very next evening, the shop was packed and very busy—which was typical being that it was Saturday. Reese had made plans to go out later that evening, so she decided that she would close out early. The clients kept rolling in, so she opted to wait on them.

She figured that she could always use more money. Noticing that she would really need to cut her shift short to get out on time, she decided that the guy that was currently in her chair was going to be her last one. He tipped her, and she began to count her slips, and total them up so she could cash out. As she was finishing up, she heard a loud crash coming from outside.

Kyle yelled, "Yo' dawg your crazy wife is out there banging up cars man! Go get her!"

Everyone jumped and looked out the window. There was a woman in the parking lot with a bat, and she was smashing it into the headlights and hood of Reese's Navigator. Reese stuffed the cash back in the drawer and grabbed a chair. She headed for the door as Shawn raced to stop her. By now, the lady with the bat was smashing out the windows to Shawn's car.

Shawn pushed Reese out of the way and ran full force to the woman, and snatched the bat from her hands.

"What the hell is wrong with you, Shay?" Shawn screamed at her. Everyone that was in the shop had begun to trickle out into the parking lot to see what was going on. Kyle was trying to pry the chair out of Reese's hands while she was screaming and cursing the whole time.

"You been sleeping with that skank!" She pointed to Reese. Reese crunched up her face and twisted up her lips. Shawn walked closer to the irate woman. *Wife?*

"Baby…c'mon now. What makes you think that?" Shawn stroked her face, and tried to convince her that she was mistaken.

"Shawn, don't try it! I saw you two last night!" Everyone gasped and started gawking at Reese. Then they turned their heads to see what Shawn was going to say.

"You saw what? Dancing? That's it! We were closing up shop, and a stepping song came on so we started dancing!" Reese's blood began to boil. *Wife?*

Shay apparently bought the story that Shawn was selling, wrapped her arms around his neck, and began to kiss him. At that moment, the chair that Reese had in her hands went flying through the air and landed in the middle of Shawn's windshield, shattering the entire thing. Everyone turned their attention to Reese with eyes spread wide in unbelief.

"Reese! What the hell did you do that for?" Shawn looked at his damaged car. Shay twisted up her face and took a step towards Reese with her fists up. Shawn knew that Reese would clobber Shay so he protected her by placing his arms in front of her to block her path.

"You had me thinking that we had to keep quiet because of your clients? I thought you just were being a private person...but you're *married!* Nigga, you married?" Reese picked up the bat that Shawn had dropped on the ground, and began to bust out Shawn's head lights. Shawn was trying to control Shay while screaming for someone to grab Reese. The guys from the shop looked at Shawn like he had just grown three heads, and backed away. Reese stopped all of a sudden, and turned to look at Shay. The crowd grew silent. "Yeah, Miss Shay. Or should I say: Mrs. Shawn Hamilton. I been sleeping with your husband! You saw exactly what you thought you saw! And that *wasn't* the first time! Tell her Shawn! Tell her how you..." Shay turned to Shawn, and slapped the hell out of him. He grabbed her with both hands and began screaming at her again. Reese was so hurt, but she absolutely *refused* to allow it to show. She figured that the reason everyone had an issue with her being overly friendly with him was because they all knew about Shay. Reese was fuming and couldn't wait to get into a shower stall *somewhere* so that she could cry. That's was the *only* place that she allowed her hurt to show aside from in the presence of her mother and Frankie—they were the *only* two beings on earth that ever saw her fragile side. She showed her anger openly, she showed her joy openly, but when it came to pain, she just refused to let anyone see her cry.

She went back inside to finish counting her tickets so that she could leave. She had called Frankie to come get her. Frankie had sounded relaxed when she answered the phone but was obviously irritated when she realized that she was going to have to come get Reese. She took a deep breath, hung up, and headed out, just the way she was dressed.

A few police cars had begun to pull into the parking lot. They immediately began to break up the crowd and restrain the hysterical Shay. Reese watched from inside as she took her commissions for the day and logged them in the ledger book at the reception desk. She walked outside and saw Anthony step out of his patrol car, and walk over to the damaged cars. When he saw her walking towards him, he realized that one of the cars belonged to her. He shook his head, and pulled out his note pad. Reese was known for her short fuse. She immediately began to defend herself because she knew what he was thinking.

"Uh-unn Tony." She said as she started shaking her index finger from side to side. "I didn't start this! That crazy mud hen just started busting out my windows!" She pointed over at Shay which set Shay off again. The police threatened to place handcuffs on her if she didn't calm down. Reese laughed and continued. "I was inside." Anthony stopped her.

"Reese, just chill. We'll take everyone's statement, and write up a report. You can take it to your insurance company, or you can press charges if you feel like it. I really don't care." He walked her away from the crowd mumbling to himself, "I ain't in the mood for drama tonight.

I'm so sick of my people acting ghetto like this…especially in public."
Anthony called over his partner, and instructed him to take Reese's
statement. When she was done telling her side of the story, she called a
tow truck to get her car, and waited for Frankie to come get her.

Frankie pulled up momentarily. Anthony was still there.
*Great…thanks Reese. I really wanted him to see me in my pajamas! You
make me sick!* She tried to avoid him because she didn't want him to see
her dressed the way she was, and besides, the sight of him always made
her feel like a fool over and over.

She left the engine running, and walked over to Reese who was
steadily fussing. *She always got something to say!* Frankie shook her
head, and Reese began to defend herself as she had with Anthony. Frankie
waved her hand because she really didn't feel like hearing it. Reese was
always raising hell somewhere or always in the middle of some kind of
drama. That particular night, Frankie really did not feel like getting up
from her couch to come out and get her. She had planned on calling it a
night early. She had taken her shower, put on her favorite pajamas,
popped her some popcorn, and wrapped up in a thick blanket on the couch
to watch one of her favorite love stories, "The Notebook."

"Hey Key-Lime. You look…comfortable." Anthony said as he
looked at her fuchsia linen pajama pants that had lime green circles
splattered all over them. He was not used to seeing her outside of a suit,
stockings, and high-heels pumps.

"Yeah…wasn't expecting to have to come out tonight." She
replied as she shot Reese an aggravated look. Reese snatched her purse
up, and walked over to Frankie's car. Frankie turned to follow her. "Have
a good one Tony. It was good seeing you…"

"It was good seeing you too Key-Lime. You look beautiful...even in your PJ's." He pulled on the leg of her pants and snickered. She smirked and waved goodbye.

During the ride back to Frankie's place, Reese told Frankie exactly what had happened as Frankie pretended to listen. The whole time, all *she* could think about was Anthony.

The sound of Frankie snapping her fingers in Reese's face caused Reese to jump, bringing her out of her daydream. She didn't realize that she had zoned out for a moment. Reese shook her head and closed her eyes briefly. "Damn him...and then tried to act brand new when it all hit the fan. Ugh!"

"Yeah...I know girl...these men...it's amazing how some of them just go through life and stomp on people's hearts without giving it a second thought. And then their comeback is that it was *just sex* and that we as women always get too emotional. I am so tired of hearing that."

"Tell me 'bout it! After Shawn hurt me like that, I just starting going *into* a relationship with the preconception that the guy wanted nothing *but* sex. I figure that, hell, if I beat them to the punch, then they can't hurt me. Those bastards do it to us! And then when they see that I ain't callin' them, or chasin' them, they can't handle it. See e're body looks at me and think I'm scandalous. But it's not like that. I'm just tired of being the one waiting by the phone."

"Wettin' the pillow with tears every night..." Frankie added.

"Goin' through all sorts of changes for them..." Reese responded.

"Being on *their* time..."

"I shut that all down a long time ago and just do my own thing. So if someone comes into my life...great...if not...who's next?"

"I'm not as strong as you Reese…you know me…a fool for love…or just a damn fool. I don't know." Frankie tossed a blanket onto Reese's lap.

"Nah…you ain't no fool girl…you just like everyone else out here…we all looking for love and becoming desperate to the point that we will devote ourselves to anything that even *looks* promising—whether it is or not."

"I know…and even *that* sounds sad." Frankie pulled her legs up on the couch and sat Indian-style.

"Well…since we talking about boo's…I met someone too." Reese giggled like a high school girl.

"Okay…do tell." Frankie tried not to cringe, but she knew that Reese had been searching online again and was pretty sure that this one was a nutcase just like the rest of them.

"Well, I don't know what he looks like just yet, except from pictures, and you can never go off that." Reese looked at Frankie knowing what she was going to ask next.

"You met him online didn't you girl?" Frankie tilted her head, and rolled her eyes.

"Yeah." Reese answered like a small child who was just about to get in trouble.

"Resse."

"I know…but this one is…"

"Different? How so? Girl, they are all crazy on there." Frankie scolded.

"I know, but…hell, I want someone to call boo sometimes too." Reese defended herself jokingly.

"And that's fine, just use a different technique. You know you always get some crazy nutty buddy when you get on that site."

"Well I'm supposed to be meeting him tomorrow so we'll see how crazy he really is. His name is Blake. He tells me he works for the F.B.I...but you know we never *really* know if they're telling the truth."

"Okay, well you know the drill."

"Yes, I know the drill, *mom*." Reese teased. The drill was to hide off in an area opposite of where you were *supposed* to really meet, and watch him from a distance. Once he was spotted, you took a picture of him with the cell phone, and immediately texted to your girls. And if you were going to be riding somewhere with him, a picture of his license plate was required as well.

They laughed and began to watch the movie.

Ten

FRANKIE WAS ENGULFED in paperwork and deep in thought. She was making great progress, and was hoping to get off early. Business was picking up, and Frankie was determined to make sure nothing slipped through the cracks. She had been receiving great feedback from her supervisors, and was adamant about keeping it that way. She had plans on meeting Greg for dinner and a movie as well, and wasn't going to miss it for the world. She and Greg had begun to form a really great relationship and couldn't seem to get enough of each other. Frankie titled her head back and swung her chair around to enjoy her view.

Patrice buzzed Frankie on the speaker phone startling her. "Frankie, can you step in here a moment please?"

"Sure. Give me just a second. In the middle of a transaction." Frankie finished up and pushed back from the desk. She walked down to the other end of the corridor and opened Patrice's door. Patrice had obviously been crying.

"What's up girl?" Frankie walked over to her and placed her hand on Patrice's trembling shoulder.

"Jackie's pregnant." Patrice burst out in tears.

"Oh Pat...I'm sorry." Frankie tried to comfort her.

"She's only sixteen Frankie. Sixteen! She's a baby herself! And she's too far along to terminate." She shouted through tears.

"Who is the father?"

"She won't tell me. I think I have an idea though. She had been hanging out with this little punk down the street. She won't talk to me and that's not like her. She tells me everything! I never saw this coming! Frankie, I know my daughters *and* my baby sisters like the back of my hands, and I never saw any change in her attitude. I mean, yeah, she's been acting like a regular teen is expected to act but nothing out of the ordinary! I don't know what to do..." Patrice buried her head in her hands and sobbed.

"Treesy, I really don't know what to say...damn...I'm sorry Patrice."

"I'm going to take the rest of the day off. I need to clear my head." Patrice grabbed a tissue and wiped her face.

"Okay girl. Take as much time as you need, I'm sure if you talk to Mike, it'll all be cool."

"I'll go talk to him...I'll be back in the morning."

Frankie watched as Patrice grabbed her things and closed up. Patrice was not only a single mother of three girls, but she had also raised her younger brothers and sisters. Their mother had disappeared altogether, and by that time Patrice and her twin, Freddie, were of age and had gone to the courts to become the legal guardians of the younger ones. Patrice took pride in the fact that she never had any trouble out of any of them. She occasionally had to get on Jackie, but nothing too extreme. She had tons

81

of framed pictures all over her office of her daughters, her sisters, and her brothers. She talked about them all the time. Patrice was a good mother and provider, considering the fact that she was young and most people expected so much less of her. Not only that, but raising six kids was hard work. This was a huge blow to Patrice. One of her goals in life was to make sure that her siblings and her daughters didn't go down the same path that she, her mother, or her father had. It was a difficult ride for her and she didn't want to see any of them struggle the way she and Freddie had. The older siblings had been there to help with the younger ones while she was in school, but it hadn't been easy. They were living comfortably now but she didn't want them to think it came easy. She wasn't always living comfortably. Patrice had struggled for years to pay the rent, put food on the table, and shoes on their feet. She had gone to bed hungry many nights so that the children could eat, and had taken on many odd jobs and not so cushy jobs to make ends meet. She loved her daughters and siblings but knew that if she would have stuck to the original plan— which was to finish school and land the job first before starting a family, then she would not have had to struggle as hard.

Frankie admired Patrice and her strength and knew that this was a big pill to swallow. Frankie had considered motherhood, but deep down knew that she wasn't ready to be a mother. Her career had become her baby. And being honest with herself, she knew that she wouldn't be able to provide a child with what they needed emotionally. Sure, she could afford to hire a nanny to raise the child for her, but how fair would that be? Frankie vowed that she would take that step once she was at a point in her career to where she would be able to work from home.

Until then, she would continue to crunch numbers. Her mother wasn't too happy that she hadn't settled down yet. She was constantly trying to introduce Frankie to the sons of various politicians, surgeons, or lawyers. Frankie would go out with a few of them on occasion to appease her mother, but for the most part, they weren't what she wanted. She was never happy with them. She always felt like she had to be someone else when she was with them. The one person that she longed to be with was Anthony, but she had thrown that opportunity out the window.

Frankie knew that her mother would probably jump for joy when she learned of her evolving romance with Greg, the world-renowned financial analyst. That would be just what she wanted for Frankie—to marry a rich man and live the high life. *Then* maybe Frankie would join them all on their Thursday morning shopping sprees.

Frankie was just finishing up as Amber buzzed her phone.

"Frankie, Greg is here."

"Send him in please." Frankie finished off a few more emails and invoices, and looked up moments later to see Greg standing there with his hands behind his back. He smiled as he presented a bouquet of tulips.

"Oh, Greg, they're gorgeous!" Frankie exclaimed.

"Well, they don't stand a chance against you. Happy six-month anniversary," he leaned over and kissed her on the cheek. Frankie blushed.

"Oh wow, can you believe it's been six months already? This year is really flying by. Let me shut my computer down and I will be ready to go." Frankie smiled back at Greg, and began to turn her computer off. She placed the flowers in an empty vase that was sitting in her window.

"You want me to grab some water for them, baby?" Greg grabbed the vase, and without receiving an answer from Frankie, he left her office and headed to the restroom. He returned with the filled vase, and placed it back in the window. Frankie smiled contently and grabbed her purse. Greg took her hands, and she followed behind.

"Have fun, kids." Amber called out as the couple left the building.

"Good night, Amber. Make sure you lock up and set the alarm."

"You got it."

After dinner Greg drove them to a park downtown not too far from the theater they were planning on going to. They walked hand-in-hand to an open space by a small pond. Lightning bugs were flickering around them, and crickets could be heard whistling.

"Are we not going to the movies?" Frankie questioned.

"Oh…yes, we're still going. I just wanted to show you my favorite spot. I like to come here and think. Isn't it beautiful in the evening?" Greg looked out over the water.

"Sure is." Frankie joined him.

"Frankie, look." Greg was now holding both of her hands and peering into her eyes.

"Yes?" Frankie's heart skipped a beat. She felt a knot grow in her stomach.

"I have really enjoyed our time together and I hope I'm not rushing anything when I say this but, I love you and I want to make a promise to you right here."

"Okay." Frankie waited to hear what he was going to say next. She hung onto his every word.

"I promise you this day that I will always be here for you. I can honestly see myself spending forever with you. And today, this night, I promise you that I will do everything in my power to secure a place in your heart forever." He then pulled out a ring from his pocket. Frankie's eyes began to water. *This is not happening! Oh my God…it is!* "This is a ring to symbolize my promise to you. For when the day comes that I ask you to be my wife, I will be confident that I have in fact secured my place

84

with you. I love you." Frankie was expecting a proposal. However, she was just as happy to receive *something*. She wooed over the ring and kissed Greg on the lips. He was such a tender hearted and romantic man. She wanted to tell him then that he had already secured his place, but she figured she would allow him to really prove himself. She was still trying to teach herself to not jump the gun and fall too hard. The rest of the evening, she couldn't keep her eyes off the ring. It was elegant and fit her tastes perfectly. *I'm finally going to be happy. Finally.*

Eleven

REESE EXAMINED THE RING on Frankie's finger and gave her approval.

"Looks real. And if this is just the promise ring, then imagine what the *real deal* is going to look like." Frankie held her hand in the air and admired the ring herself for the thousandth time. She wasn't quite ready for marriage and a family, but this was good, for now. This felt good to her.

She could see herself as Greg's wife. They clicked. They enjoyed the same things and were both committed to the success of their careers. They both enjoyed traveling and sightseeing. He loved to cook and she loved to sit and watch him perform miracles in the kitchen. He was an awesome chef. He would lay and paint Frankie's toenails as she worked on her laptop. She would fly out to visit him whenever he left on one of his many business trips because he would call and tell her that he was lonely, and missing her. He was charming, and the love they made was always hot and heavy. Frankie felt like she was suffocating whenever he would be gone for long periods of time. She had completely let her guard down and really believed that this would finally be the missing piece to her puzzled life.

"So, how's *your* cyber-love life coming?" Frankie joked.

"Pretty good. Got a lot of irons in the fire. My hopes are that I can recognize all the red flags and eliminate one by one, until I find the one for me." Frankie just shook her head chuckling. Reese continued. "Well you know I been seeing Blake for a while now…been like six or seven months."

"Yeah, how's that going? You don't talk about him much. When do I get to meet him? Since it *has* been almost a year."

"Oh I know…every time we all try to get together, something always seems to come up. I'm sure we will all get together real soon because I would love to meet Greg in person. So far, I approve of him dating my best friend." Reese winked at Frankie. "But, it's going really good." Reese sounded as if she was trying to convince herself of it. "I guess."

"You guess? What's wrong with him?"

"He works so much. We text a lot and chat online more than anything. It has really gotten old, and I'm bout ready to drop him. You know me."

"Yep…that's why we call you hotcakes."

"Cause I be droppin' 'em like hotcakes!" Reese stood up and squatted to the ground laughing.

"Girl, you crazy."

"I'm serious as hell. These fools keep it up and I'ma be getting it on with your cousin June Bug."

"Girl, please. June Bug is not trying to get involved. He knows that ya'll hookahs only out for his money. He ain't dumb."

"Well, hell I think I got a better chance at landing him. Put in a good word for me girl." Reese pleaded. Frankie snickered.

"I'm meeting him for breakfast tomorrow anyways. I'll feel him out for you." Frankie said as she lay across the couch. Reese laughed but deep inside she was not content with Frankie's response.

Twelve

FRANKIE STOOD IN THE middle of the café entrance, and scanned the room for her cousin. He was off to the right on his cell phone, of course. She walked up to the table and sat down. He put up his index finger and finished his call. Frankie glanced over the menu as she waited. He put his phone down and leaned over to kiss his favorite cousin on the cheek.

"Hey, Tweety. Muah!" He sat back down and picked up the menu.

"Hey, Bug. You stay working huh?"

"You should talk."

"Yeah, guess you right."

"I *know* I'm right. That was a client of mine who is driving me up the wall. She calls non-stop! She is trying to catch her husband cheating and wants to know the best way to do it so that it all stands up in court."

"What?" Frankie laughed.

"Yes. I deal with this everyday." His phone went off again. He ignored the call. "Let me put this phone on silent or we will *never* get to talk." June fumbled with the phone and then placed it in the holster on his hip.

"I bet. How's Aunt Lisa doing?" Frankie waved for the waitress.

"She's good. You know how it goes. Her and Pops always going at it." They both laughed.

The waitress showed up and took their orders. Frankie then thought about her conversation with Reese. She knew that June would look at her like she was crazy but she asked anyways.

"How would you feel about me hooking you up with a girlfriend of mine?"

"Frankie, I am *not* going out with Reese."

"June! What's wrong with Reese?" Frankie grinned. She already knew.

"Frankie, please. You know what's wrong with her. She's off the chain! I'm just going to be real and say it up front, I can't handle her. She's too much for me." He admitted. Frankie left it alone, and felt better for at least attempting. That way she wouldn't have to lie when Reese cornered her about it later.

June and Frankie enjoyed a heated, yet friendly political debate about the presidential candidates for the upcoming election, over a delectable breakfast of poached eggs, bacon, bagels, fruit, and pancakes.

June waved the waitress down to get the check. They finished up their conversation and hugged each other. June was meeting a client at the office and had to get going, and Frankie needed to get to the office to prepare for some upcoming presentations with a few highly esteemed clients. Frankie's promotion was riding on her ability to acquire these important clients' accounts. Just as they stepped outside, June was approached by a shorter woman, with auburn colored hair. She had three children in tow, and was obviously angry.

"Mister Matthews! I have been trying to call you all morning!" She was obviously a client.

"Mrs. Taylor, I understand but you and I were supposed to be meeting at my office in fifteen minutes. It's not time for our meeting yet. I was having breakfast with family." He pointed over at Frankie. Frankie was standing off to the side—staring in amusement with a grin on her face. This must have been the client he was talking about that was driving him insane. June turned to Frankie. "Kiekie, call me later. Love you." He kissed her on the cheek and grabbed the irate lady by the arm. The lady looked back at Frankie.

"I'm sorry for interrupting." The lady called back as June led her down the street to his office, assuring her that everything was okay.

Thirteen

REESE STOOD OUTSIDE the department store admiring the hot pink stilettos. She was going to finally try to be more ladylike, and try a pair. She built up enough courage to walk into the store, and phoned Frankie.

"Hey Reese Cup!" Frankie cried happily.

"Hey Kie. Look. Pray for me."

"What? What's the matter?" Frankie's voice changed to panic.

"No...calm down. I'm in Listrani's about to try on a pair of three inches."

Frankie laughed. "Let me know how that works out for you. Call me if you need me to get you from the hospital."

"Real funny. Cow." She flipped her phone shut, and waited for a representative to assist her. She sat her bag down, and glanced around the room. There were tons of shoes that she was ready to try on. She was tired of men giving her off-the-wall excuses for why they figured things wouldn't work out. Reese knew that she was a gorgeous woman, but she had a tough time letting go of her tom-boy, street side—which was intimidating to men.

Reese noticed a younger girl trying on a pair of flats. The girl stood up, and walked over to a mirror to check them out. Reese watched her as the girl lifted one foot, and then the other. The girl sat back down, and placed the shoes back in the box. She noticed Reese looking at her.

"Hi." The girl smiled. Reese smiled back, and quickly turned her head to look for a representative. "My feet are killing me in these high-heels." The girl said as she tried on another pair of ballerina flats. "Had to down grade to flats." She slid one foot out of the shoe, propped her foot up on her leg, and began to massage it. Her feet were red, and swollen. This made Reese think twice about wearing those heels.

A representative came over and asked Reese if she had been helped. Reese responded and was then asked to wait as they rang up the girl with the flats. The girl noticed the high-heels in Reese's hand.

"Good luck," she whispered as she walked to the register to check out. Reese nodded and smiled nervously.

Reese tried on about fifteen different shoes until she found a pair that fit her perfectly. They were comfortable and worth every dime. As the clerk rang up her purchase, Reese wandered off towards the front of the store to admire the hot pink ones again. As she reached down to grab them, she looked up to see Blake coming out of the café from across the street. He was talking to the young girl that had just bought the flats not too long ago. Reese thought he was in Cleveland on business. She grabbed the hot pink shoes, and asked the clerk to ring them up for her as well. While they went to locate Reese's size, she turned her attention back to Blake and the young girl outside. She couldn't tell what was happening exactly, but then noticed the girl throw her hands up in the air and walk off. She looked like she was crying. Blake shook his head and hailed down a cab.

The clerk completed Reese's sale, handed her the bags and receipt. Reese thanked her, and headed out the store just in time to make eye contact with Blake. He looked guilty, but didn't stop. He climbed in the cab and disappeared down 13th Street.

Reese told herself that she wasn't going to call him. She knew that he had seen her, and she was going to leave the ball in his court. She was tired of being lied to and was sick of playing games. Most men called her aggressive. Some called her flat out mean and hard to please. June called her off the chain. It wasn't that she was hard to please. It was that she just wasn't going to allow these men to alter her sanity in any way shape or form. She had had her share of drama and pain, and had decided to just live and let live. *Easy come, easy go.* Sure, she didn't want to be lonely, who did? But she also didn't want to spend her time chasing after a man regardless of how great she may have thought he was. It wasn't long after she thought this that her phone rang. It was Blake.

"Reese, I know you saw me today." He sounded guilty.

"Um-hmm." Reese mumbled.

"I just got back from Cleveland, and I was meaning to call you. I was going to surprise you baby. But you busted me!" He laughed nervously.

"Okay. But who was that girl you were talking to?" Blake was thinking of a good answer. *Damn, she really saw me.*

"That was my niece," he said, hoping that Reese would buy it.

"Your niece huh?" She didn't buy it.

"Yeah. I was fussing at her because she should have been at school and was out shopping. That's why you may have seen her walk off

94

crying. She doesn't like it when I get onto her," he explained. Reese let it go. But she still wasn't satisfied with his answer. She felt like he had already said too much—which was a clear indicator that he was lying. She didn't remember him ever talking about siblings or family that lived around there. And besides, why was he that far from the airport if he had just gotten back? Something wasn't right and Reese could feel it. She wasn't one to go investigating anything or snooping around, she just didn't have the energy for that type of stuff anymore. She loved to lay and wait, and let Karma have her way. Because eventually what is done in the dark will come to light.

Fourteen

THE MUSIC FILLED the air, and she felt as though they were the only ones on the dance floor. Frankie placed her head on Greg's chest. He was wearing her favorite cologne. She took a long deep whiff of it. She wanted to stay there in his arms forever. He placed his hands on the small of her back and pulled her in closer. She closed her eyes, and imagined what life would be like when they finally did decide to take the next step towards marriage. Maybe she *was* ready for a family. After all, she *was* landing more top-dollar accounts, and had received tremendous reviews on her performance. She felt that her biological clock *was* ticking. She was happy though, that she was still in a position where she could make that decision on her own and not have it made for her.

"Frankie, you look like an angel tonight." Greg whispered in her ear. "The day I make you my wife is going to be the happiest day of my life. I'm a lucky man." Frankie exhaled, and wondered when he would actually pop the question. She wouldn't dare ask him, or ask him when he was going to ask her. She didn't want to seem desperate, even though she longed to be in a truly committed relationship. She was tired of the dating game. She always seemed to be the one losing. They danced on another slow song, and then went back to their seats to enjoy a light dinner and wine.

As they listened to the band play, Frankie studied Greg's facial features intently. She noticed his lips, and how soft they were. She smiled because just as soft as his lips were, so were the kind words that always fell from them. She looked at his eyes, which always looked back at her with so much admiration that made her feel like royalty. She looked at his ears; they were perfectly shaped, and she thought of the many nights that she lay on his chest and poured out her soul sharing her dreams with him as he used those perfectly shaped ears to listen to her. She moved her focus then to his arms. They were so firm and muscular—not too much, but just right. They were perfect for her. They held her just right and always made her feel safe. She then looked at his hands. They were much larger than hers, and they were so soft and smooth, just like his lips. She thought of how she loved when he would stroke her cheek as he stared into her eyes. She thought of how sometimes he would just grab her hand just to hold it in his.

He changed positions in his seat and her eyes shifted to his chest. It was always so warm and inviting, and she couldn't get enough of touching it and laying her head on it. Greg noticed that she was looking at him and turned his head towards her.

"Something wrong, baby?" He asked as he placed those strong arms around her shoulders.

"Oh, no baby. I was just admiring you." Greg laughed quietly and then leaned over and kissed her on the cheek.

"There's nothing to admire, boo." He squeezed her shoulders. "Are you enjoying yourself, baby?"

"Yes, I am. This is really nice. I never knew this club was here. My best friend has an awesome voice. I would love to see her up on stage singing along with a band. "

"Oh yeah?"

"Yeah, she only sings in front of me. She doesn't believe that she's got a unique sound. But I try to encourage her every now and then. I think that one day she may take my advice and finally give in. I'm really going to have to bring her here. It's really nice."

"It's my little secret. I like to come here to just get away, you know?" Greg closed his eyes, and moved his head to the sensual beats of Unison, the featured jazz band that was currently playing one of their hits. "What do you say to going on a European Cruise with me this summer?"

"Sounds like fun. Just tell me when." Frankie jumped with delight on the inside. *This must be when he plans on proposing!* And Frankie was so ready to say "yes." Everyday that she spent with him, she fell more and more in love with him. The more she thought about it, the more confident she was in making that choice to commit. She held his hand tighter, and imagined herself as his wife, again, and let the soft jazz take her away.

Fifteen

ON THE WAY HOME from the romantic evening with Greg, Frankie called Reese as she drove back to her place.

"Girl he's going to pop the question!" Frankie screamed. Reese sounded unimpressed.

"How do you figure? I'm not hatin', I just don't understand why he hasn't yet. I mean, yeah, you got a promise ring, but…"

"Reese, please just be happy for me. You know what I've been through."

"Yes, Frankie, I have been there from the beginning, I just don't want you to expect it and then get your feelings hurt. I love you girl, that's all." Reese paused. "Let me ask…are you happy?"

"Yes."

"Truly happy…not with Greg, but with yourself."

"Yes." Frankie never thought about it. She *figured* she was happy with herself. She was definitely happy with Greg. Reese knew that Frankie didn't understand the question. She let it go.

"Then I'm happy. When you hurt, I hurt and you know that. When you smile, I smile."

"Yes, I know."

"Just don't have me in a crazy looking bridesmaid dress!" Reese teased. Frankie laughed.

"So how are things going with you and Blake?" Frankie hadn't heard Reese talk about him.

"I don't know girl. Something is funny, but you know me, I ain't going to ask any questions. Because it will all come out in the wash."

"Well, what happened?"

"I can't really call it right now, but I think he's been lying about being on his business trips. I think he may be seeing someone else, but I am not going to get too caught up in it. Easy come, easy go." Reese was the stronger one of them two. She *had* a heart but was very careful who she let in. Frankie, on the other hand, was so willing to give everyone a chance. She always believed that she should let her pain from previous relationships stay in the past and not bring them to the next relationship by making the new person pay. Reese giggled, and asked about her number one love interest. "So, what's June up to these days? Did you ask him about me?"

"Girl, he is fine. And yes, I asked him about you. He told me that he couldn't handle you." Frankie laughed.

"He can't *handle* me? What that hell does that mean?"

"You see! Right there, that attitude. You always so ready to fight." Frankie laughed. She loved when Reese got fired up, at times. She tried to picture June and Reese together, and laughed at the thought. Although, they did make a cute couple on the outside, they were two totally different people. Reese was a hairstylist, and June was a lawyer.

100

Reese was loud; June was reserved. Reese always spoke her mind, never holding her tongue. June was more conservative and dated women who rarely said anything. All the women that Frankie had ever met that June dated were all alike. But for whatever reasons, they never worked out.

Surprisingly, Reese accepted what Frankie had to say. "You know I have been trying to get it under control." Reese's voice saddened.

Frankie noticed the change in her tone, "Girl, you fine. June is just used to the same old stuff. You know, those real prissy, dry type girls. You are unique, boo-boo," Frankie said in baby talk. Reese sucked her teeth and giggled. "Girl, speaking of June, I need to stop by there tomorrow and drop something off for my Aunt. You wanna hang?"

"You ain't said nothin' but a word!"

"I figured as much. I'm leaving at eight."

"I'll be there at seven!"

The next morning, Reese was walking through the door at seven o'clock on the dot. That was one thing that Frankie *could* say about her best friend. She was prompt when it came to something she wanted. They rode the subway down to 23rd Street, and walked up the sidewalk to June's office. As they walked in, a young black girl wearing a really short haircut called out.

"Hello. Can I help you?" she said without looking up from her computer screen.

"Hi. Mr. Matthews please?" Frankie said as she approached the counter. Reese sat down in the waiting room chairs and crossed her legs. Frankie laughed to herself at the sight of Reese trying to hide her inner tomboy who was probably choking at that moment.

"He's in with a client right now. And I'm not sure how much longer he will be."

"I'm his cousin, Frankie Le—"

"Oh! Ms. Leone! So nice to meet you! I have heard so much about you!" The girl stood up and grabbed Frankie's hand.

"Oh, well I hope it has all been good." Frankie looked back at Reese with a smirk on her face.

"I will page him for you. He's in with that Mrs. Taylor, so I'm sure he won't mind." The girl began to press numbers on her phone just as a door from the back opened. She stopped dialing. "Oh, looks like they are done now." She pointed to the hallway, and Frankie chose to sit next to Reese, and wait for June to walk out.

Minutes later, June appeared with the lady from the café, Mrs. Taylor. She had her three children with her again. When she spotted Frankie, she smiled. "I remember you. From the café. I was *just* leaving so now you can have your man all to yourself sweetie. Ya'll do make a cute lil' couple." She turned and eyed June with a huge smile as if she was giving her approval.

"Uh, Mrs. Taylor, this is my cousin, Frankie." Mrs. Taylor looked like she knew she had just placed her foot in her mouth. She smiled sheepishly and reached out her hand.

"I do apologize honey. Nice to meet you." At that moment, Reese stood up and walked over. Frankie then introduced Reese.

"And *this* is my best friend, Reese." Reese smiled and shook hands.

"Well...nice to meet you." Mrs. Taylor turned to June, "I guess I will be off now. As always, thank you. I will be calling you shortly to touch base. Ya'll have a great day!" And she walked out the door with her three children following close behind like a mother duck walking cross the street. June looked frazzled as he waved goodbye.

"Man! She's a character, huh?" June said as he led Frankie and Reese back to the waiting area. He tried his best to ignore Reese's overly exaggerated attempts to be prissy, but he had to laugh to himself, because he found it hilarious, and sort of cute.

"Here's the information that your mom wanted. Tell her she can call whenever she's ready for a presentation." Frankie held out a booklet that gave detailed information regarding the services that Wallace Nvest offered. Her aunt was trying to open a new branch of her bank, and had seriously been considering switching investment accounts. She wanted to use Frankie's expertise in the process.

They all stood up and June, because he *was* a gentleman, hugged them both, and walked them to the door. It wasn't that he didn't *like* Reese—he thought she was gorgeous and funny. It was more so that he looked at her as a kid sister. Reese *was* over the top for him, he just never considered any titles other than "kid-sister" or even "play cousin" when it came to Reese.

When they got to the car, Reese was floating on air. Had she actually been chocolate, she would have melted right there. She periodically sniffed her collar where June's cologne had rested from when he hugged her.

Sixteen

FRANKIE WAS FEELING very confident about the meeting she had just had with Porter & Robertson, Inc. They were one of the largest engineering firms and were rapidly expanding. They were on Frankie's hot-list, and she would be sure to earn a hefty bonus *and* promotion if she was successful in capturing them as official clients. They were in the market for a more promising investment and retirement plan for their employees, and Frankie's presentation had honestly, by far, been the best one they had seen. She felt confident that she was going to win their business. Not only would she be responsible for procuring this account, she would be the main point of contact for all future transactions, and Porter & Robertson were well known for providing generous referrals— which meant more business for Wallace NVest.

She left their office and headed straight for hers to deliver the great news to Mike who would probably jump about five feet into the air. Frankie laughed at the thought. She stepped off the subway and walked one block to her company's building. She stepped into the lobby and was just about to scan her identification card when she noticed Jackie sitting off in the waiting area reading a book about what she could expect to happen to her body during the pregnancy. Frankie walked over and sat next to her. Jackie looked up and smiled.

"Hi, Ms. Frankie."

"Hey sweetie. How are you feeling today? Your sister said that you had been having some morning sickness." Frankie leaned over and rubbed Jackie's stomach.

"I'm feeling better these days. I'm just ready to have this baby." She sounded exhausted.

"I hear that...I'll go check on Patrice and let her know you're here." Frankie stood up and went up to Patrice's office. Patrice was on the floor with files and papers sprawled out everywhere.

"Wow...Hurricane Patrice!" Frankie joked.

"Girl, I'm trying to calculate all our P&L for the Mitchell Group. What's up?" Patrice didn't even look up from the sea of papers.

"Jackie is downstairs."

Patrice stopped what she was doing and smacked her hand to her head. "Oh my God! She has an appointment today! I completely forgot." Patrice looked at the sea of papers and then closed her eyes in thought. Frankie knew how much Patrice hated interrupting her flow.

"I'll take her for you." Frankie offered.

"Oh, Frankie, would you? That would be so good. Thank you. Thank you. Thank you! Here, take my car." Patrice reached up on her desk and grabbed her keys. She tossed them to Frankie and went back to punching numbers on the calculator.

"Go head and get back to what you were doing. Tell Mike I'll be back shortly if he asks." Frankie turned to walk out and Patrice blew her a kiss. Frankie and Jackie walked out to the parking lot and got into

Patrice's car. Traffic was lighter during that time of the day. Frankie turned the radio up a little bit and began to groove to an old school jam that reminded her of her unforgettable summers back in the day.

"Ms. Frankie?" Jackie said, peering out the passenger side window as they stopped at a light.

"Yes."

"I'm scared."

"Well boo…" Frankie thought that this would be a great opportunity to get Jackie to talk since she was refusing to tell her sister anything. Sometimes teenagers will confide in someone else that they feel they can trust. And it's not that they don't trust their parents, or guardians for that matter, it's just that they may not want to hear all the yelling and screaming once they do decide to confide them. Frankie could totally relate. "You're having a baby, and you're just a baby yourself."

"I know…" she whispered softly. "I didn't mean for this to happen." She said almost as if she was pleading to Frankie. "I told him no…" Frankie's heart dropped. Frankie took a second to gather her thoughts.

"What are you saying J?" Frankie pulled over to the side of the road as cars flew past honking their horns and screaming out profanities. Jackie lowered her head and began to cry. "J! Please honey, talk to me!" Frankie's heart began to race. Jackie continued to cry. Frankie placed her hand on Jackie's chin and turned her head to face her. "J, I will not look at you any differently than I did the day when your mother brought you home from the hospital. She laid you in your big sister's arms while we were there studying. I fell in love with you then, and I love you now, boo. You did nothing wrong. Please tell me why you are crying. Please J." Frankie's eyes filled with tears as she pleaded for Jackie to tell all.

Between her tears, Jackie tried to explain. "I shouldn't have gone over there, but I did." Frankie wanted to ask her: what she was talking about. But she kept her mouth shut and prayed that Jackie would keep talking. She did. "I met this guy online. He told me that he liked my picture, and that I was cute." Jackie was sniffling and trying to catch her breath. "He told me that he loved me, Ms. Frankie." Jackie looked up and the expression in her eyes told Frankie that she really believed that guy did love her. "I thought he loved me!" Frankie began to rub her back. "He gave me a hotel room number at the La Plata and told me that he wanted to show me how much he loved me." Frankie continued rubbing Jackie's back with one hand and wiping her tears with her other. "So…I went…you know, I thought it was going to be like in the movies. I thought we would have dinner and movies and chocolate covered strawberries…you know…like in the movies." She kept crying and Frankie continued to rub. Jackie looked up at Frankie.

"Yes, I know what you mean…like the movies." Frankie felt like she was walking on eggshells. But she kept her comments very short. She was determined to get Jackie to talk.

"Well, when I walked in the room, he grabbed me and threw me on the bed. I asked him to stop and he just kept saying that he was going to make a woman out of me. 'I'm going to make a woman out of you girl!' is what he kept saying…then," Jackie took a deep breath. Frankie encouraged her to keep going and told her that it was okay. "Then, he…ripped my panties off…and…and," Jackie began to cry uncontrollably.

"Wait right here sweetie." Frankie opened the door and ran inside the convenient store that she had pulled up in front of. She ran inside and grabbed a bottle of water and a chocolate bar. She paid for the items and ran back to the car. "Here baby, drink some water." She opened the bottle and handed it to Jackie.

She took a sip. "I'm sorry Ms. Frankie. I'm so sorry."

"J, it is *not* your fault, honey. That guy is a monster and we need to make sure that he doesn't do this to any other girls. We have to tell, J."

"I don't want to get him in trouble!" Jackie pleaded.

"J, look at you. You are in pieces, honey. Think about your nieces!" Jackie looked at Frankie in horror. "Yes, think about, Kayla, Cierra and Kendra. What if he did the same thing to them!"

"I wouldn't want that…" Jackie looked out the window as more tears began to fall. "All I know is that he goes by the name of Tae."

"Sweetie, that's good enough."

Seventeen

PATRICE LOOKED AT HER baby sister.

"Raped?" Patrice stared in disbelief as Frankie explained to her what she had just discovered. Patrice grabbed Jackie and pulled her in close. She hugged her tightly and began to sob. "I'm going to kill the monster that did this to you! Wait 'til I tell Freddie! Frankie, you need to go ahead and tell Junebug, that I am going to need his services. Cause I'm going to jail!"

"Treesy, calm down, hon. No one is going to die. You are not going to kill anyone. And you damn sure ain't going to jail!" Frankie placed her arms around the sobbing and trembling woman. She could only imagine the sense of violation that one would feel if their flesh and blood had been robbed of their innocence. "We *can* make sure that he does not ever do this to anyone else again though. I have a friend down at the police station. We have to go and press charges, and he will make sure that your case gets handled properly. We have to tell. You remember Tony, don't you?"

"Tony D? Of course, I remember." Patrice began to control her breathing. "Okay. Okay," Patrice said calmly. She released Jackie and stood up. "Okay. J-bird, let's get 'em."

Eighteen

BY THE TIME Frankie, Patrice and Jackie had arrived at the station, Reese was waiting for them. Reese had wanted to be there as additional support when she heard that Patrice was in trouble. The moment that Jackie and Reese saw each other, they crunched up their eyebrows. It had been years since Reese had last seen Jackie. However, she recognized her from somewhere else.

"Hey Treesy...how are you feeling girl?" Reese asked while hugging Patrice and staring at Jackie.

"I'll be fine once this demon is behind bars!" Reese hugged Frankie and kissed her on the cheek. She then turned her attention to Jackie as Frankie and Patrice walked up to the front counter to ask for Lt. Davis.

"You look...so familiar...I can't put my finger on it." Jackie said to Reese as Reese studied Jackie's face closely. She then looked her up and down and recognized her instantly. "The shoe store!" Jackie snapped her fingers and pointed at Reese, "Yep. I remember you now." Reese immediately remembered where she had seen Jackie. Reese was now even more curious as to why Jackie was talking to Blake outside the café that morning.

"Yeah, I saw you not too soon after that day you bought those shoes. You were talking to your uncle. I know him very well." Jackie's expression changed.

"That wasn't my uncle." Jackie snapped. Just before Reese could say anything else, Anthony entered the lobby and greeted everyone. As he opened the double doors, a draft caused everyone's clothes to cling to their bodies momentarily. Jackie's belly poked out and Reese's mouth dropped.

Anthony escorted them to the back. Reese opted to stay in the lobby with her thoughts. *No way! He couldn't be sleeping with her! She's a minor! And she's pregnant!*

Reese paced back and forth as she waited for Frankie to come out of the office. She wanted to call Blake and let him know that she was on to him and let him know that she was going to the authorities to report that he was sleeping with a minor. Reese was so overwhelmed that she became impatient, and pulled out her phone. She dialed Blake's number. There was no answer, as usual. She didn't leave a message. She sat down and patted her foot as her mind began to race. She wasn't even hurt, she was pissed and she was going to let it show. *You done messed with the wrong one Mr. Blake!*

About an hour had passed. Reese had stopped pacing and was sitting patiently on the bench near the exit doors. She leaned her head up against the wall and looked around the station. There were police at their desks taking statements from various people. Some were writing, or on the phone. At one point, a few cops came bursting through the front doors with a man in handcuffs who was kicking and screaming. He had tattoos all over his body and he was ranting and raving about it not being his

112

fault—whatever *it* was. Reese was just about to go check the vending machine for a snack when the doors from the back swung open and Anthony, Frankie, Patrice and Jackie appeared. Patrice was holding Jackie as they thanked Anthony, and walked together outside. Frankie stopped to thank Anthony as well. Reese stood off to the side impatiently waiting for Frankie to finish talking to Anthony.

"I really appreciate what you're doing for us, Tony." Frankie touched him on the arm.

"Frankie, you know me. I'll do anything for you. And this is my passion, putting crooks behind bars and off my streets. Tell Patrice that I will turn the drawing over to our investigators and they will put it out there. Once he's on the wanted list, it won't be long before we catch him. Ask Jackie to try and get more information on him that would be helpful. Maybe she can get him to tell her more than just a nickname, and we may have a better chance at catching this asshole. Also, tell Patrice to call me if she doesn't hear from me by tomorrow evening."

"I sure will." Frankie grabbed his card and placed it in her purse. "Thank you, Tony."

"You're most welcome. You look beautiful, as always, I must say." Frankie thanked him again and reached for Reese's hand. They both walked out to catch up with Patrice and Jackie. Before they stepped completely outside, Reese stopped Frankie in her tracks and pulled her close.

"What's up, Reese?" Frankie sounded annoyed.

"Blake *has* been cheating!" She talked in a low tone as she looked outside.

"Really? Damn, Reese. I'm sorry." Frankie tried to break away from Reese's grip but Reese pulled her tighter. "Dammit Reese, hold on!

Let me take care of Patrice and Jackie right quick." Frankie tried to snatch away again but Reese clutched even harder. "Reese! What?"

"Dammit Frankie, just listen to me! He's been cheating on me!" Reese was about three inches from Frankie's face.

"Yes, we know that now! He's been cheating. Can we please talk about this back at my place?"

"Frankie, I think he's been doing it with Jackie!" Frankie's face changed to a pale yellow. She looked as if she had seen a ghost and hit the lottery at the same time.

"What? Blake?" Frankie looked out the door at Jackie. "That son of a bitch! He's the one we are looking for, I bet!"

"Looking for? Looking for him for what?"

"Reese, c'mon. Where have *you* been for the past two hours? Look at Jackie. She's pregnant and she just told us that she was raped by some dude named Tae that she met online." Frankie explained.

"And what does that have to do with Blake?" Reese was confused. Frankie was becoming frustrated.

"Ok, wait. How do you know it's Blake?" Frankie asked.

"I just know…okay. I saw them two talking outside that day I went to Listrani's and tried on those heels. Jackie was at the shoe store. You know I haven't seen Jackie since God knows when. So it's not like I *knew* who she really was."

"You saw *Blake* talking to *Jackie*?" Frankie asked as she released herself from Reese's grip.

"Yes." Frankie pulled Reese with her and they stepped outside.

"Jackie?" Frankie yelled loudly as she stepped down onto the sidewalk. Jackie turned to Frankie. "Do you remember talking to a man

outside the café across from Listrani's the day you ran into Reese, here?"
Frankie pointed to Reese. Jackie looked Reese in the eyes.

"Yes." She lowered her head.

"Who was that?" Frankie asked desperately. Jackie didn't
respond. "Jackie, who was that?" Frankie grabbed her by the shoulders
and forced her to look into her eyes.

"Jackie, girl you better speak up!" Patrice yelled.

"It was Tae okay! It was Tae!" Jackie burst into tears.

Nineteen

PATRICE TOOK THE NEXT day off and chose to stay at home by the phone with Jackie. Frankie sat in her office and tried her best to concentrate on her next presentation. It was so hard for her to think straight with knowing that her best friends were in pain and that sweet teenager was suffering with the effects that accompany rape and pregnancy. She picked up the phone and gave Reese a call.

"Hey mama, how you feeling?" Frankie questioned as she began to doodle her name and Greg's on the notepad by her phone.

"I'm good, babe. You know me!" Reese sounded like she was honestly trying to convince herself that she was okay.

"Well, I was just checking on you. You feel like some take-out tonight? My treat?"

"Hell yeah! I'll be here. Pick up a good movie too. We ain't done that in a while."

"Got'cha…I have to run by the courthouse to take care of some business. After that I'll be on my way." Frankie hung up and then dialed

116

Greg. It went straight to voicemail. "Hey baby, it's me. I just needed to call and let you know that I will not be available tonight. I've got a girlfriend in the pits and I'm going to spend some time with her tonight. Call me when you get this. Bye." Frankie hung up the phone and grabbed her purse and keys. She headed for the courthouse.

She was about one block away and her phone rang. It was Greg.

"Hey baby…just got your message."

"Good. Well, I'm not going to be at your fingertips tonight baby, but oh how I would like to." Frankie teased him.

"Well it's all good. Call me when you get home tonight. I'm bout to step into a meeting. Love you."

"Love you too!" Frankie placed the phone in her purse and stepped out the car. She climbed the steps and bumped into June.

"Hey Cuz!" June kissed her on the cheek.

"Hey Bug. You is a hard working brotha I tell you!" Frankie joked.

"Yeah…that's what I do best…hey…Patrice called me. She told me about her baby sister and Reese. How are they doing?"

"Well you know Reese. She's the come-back kid. She don't let much faze her. But Patrice and Jackie are having a hard time. They are waiting for the cops to find Blake. They've been searching for him since last night, so it's still early, I guess."

"Yeah, but our Police are good. They will find him. And since you got Tony over there heading up things, it won't be long before they snag him. What are you doing up here?"

"Oh, I'm turning in some business license application stuff for Mike. Then heading to Reese's for Chinese and a chick flick."

June laughed. "Well give crazy ole' Reese a kiss on the cheek for me. She tries to act hard, but I know she's really soft."

"Yeah, I will. How long you going to be up here?" Frankie started walking towards the metal detector.

"Oh, please, who knows? I'm in with Mrs. Taylor. This is the day we've all been waiting for. We're on break right now. Once this divorce is final, I hope I never hear from her again." Frankie and June just laughed. June hugged his favorite cousin, and then walked back into the courtroom.

Frankie walked up the steps to the licensing office to turn in the paperwork. By the time she was finished, the courthouse was just about to close. She was making good time. She planned to go straight to Video Joe's and grab a flick, and then to Won-Ton's Chinese Cuisine and grab some take-out. She pulled her cell phone out of her purse and she began to walk down the courthouse steps. The court must have been adjourning because she saw the door fling open and June appeared back in the lobby with an overly ecstatic Mrs. Taylor. She was laughing and dancing all the way to the door. June was smiling and shaking his head. Frankie bumped June when she got to the bottom of the stairs and smiled.

"Thank God! It is over! I'm going to go have me a drink!" June hugged Frankie and began to follow Mrs. Taylor out. Just then a loud voice ruptured from behind Frankie.

"That's fine Lillian! You think this is over! This shit ain't over!" Frankie recognized that voice. She turned to see Greg standing there with the three children Mrs. Taylor carried around with her all the time. Anger was written all over his face. Frankie dropped everything, including her heart.

Twenty

FRANKIE SPED THROUGH town as she dialed Reese's number. *Pick up Reese! Dammit!*

"Sup hookah. You got my fried rice?" Reese sounded like she had been sleeping.

"Get up! Wake the hell up Reese! Get your things and meet me at my place right now! I'm taking a trip to the cabin and I don't want to be alone, and I'll be damned if I'm bringing a MAN with me!" Frankie's other line beeped. It was Greg.

"What the f'—Reese sat up off the couch and rubbed her eyes.

"Girl, it's a long story! But all I can say is that Greg and I are done!" Frankie tried to hold back the tears.

"What? What? What happened Frankie?"

"That bastard is married!" Frankie began to cry even more. *"And got three damn kids!"* Frankie was screaming frantically.

"What?…damn Frankie! I'm so sorry…I'll whoop his ass!" Reese was screaming too. She could handle when her own heart hurt, but when it was Frankie, that was another story.

"Reese, just pack your things and come on."

"Be there in fifteen." Reese slammed the phone down and ran to pack her things. Frankie's phone continued to ring. By the time she got to her home, she had twelve missed calls from Greg. She sat in her car and began to wail. Her heart hurt so bad that it felt like someone was actually squeezing it. Her phone continued to vibrate in her lap. Annoyed, she flipped it open and screamed as loud as she could in the receiver, "You son of a bitch! I hope you burn in hell!" And she slammed it down. The phone rang again. She looked at the display screen. Her vision was blurred from the tears. It was Anthony. Guilt fell on her shoulders instantly. She was reminded that she wouldn't be sitting there in tears, screaming into her phone, had she not been so shallow and selfish years ago.

"Hello." She tried to choke back the tears.

"Damn, Key-lime, what did I do?" Anthony responded. He was confused.

"Huh?" Frankie was out of sorts as well.

"You just called me an S.O.B. What did I do?"

"Oh my God, Tony! I thought you were someone else. I'm sorry." Frankie apologized and laid her head back on the chair. Her head was pounding. She looked in the rear view mirror and noticed that her eyes were red, swollen and puffy.

"Messing with those punks again I see." He said in a sort of see-you-should-have-stayed-with-me type tone.

"Tony, please." Frankie had beaten herself up enough and wasn't in the mood to hear how bad she had hurt him years ago.

"Ok Key-lime. Look, I couldn't get Patrice to answer her phone. I wanted to let you all know that we just arrested the perpetrator about five minutes ago. We have him in custody and they will be bringing him in for questioning within the next thirty minutes. We need Jackie to come and pick him out of the line-up."

"Sure." Frankie wiped her face. Sniffling, "I'll take care of it. I'll call you when we are on our way." Frankie hung up the phone and called Patrice's home phone. Cierra answered.

"Cece! Hey cutie! Where's your mom?"

"Uh, hey Ms. Frankie! Hold on. MAMAAAAA!!! MS. FRANKIE ON THE PHONE!!!! She comin' Ms. Frankie." Frankie chuckled to herself. Those girls always made her laugh. Frankie explained to Patrice what was going on and agreed to meet them at the station in thirty minutes.

Frankie got on the elevator to go up to her home and Reese yelled from behind her to get her to hold the door. Reese jogged with a gym bag on her shoulder and jumped between the closing doors.

"Hey boo." Reese hugged Frankie. Reese had a serious look on her face that typically meant she was ready to fight. The doors opened and Reese opted to stay there and hold them while Frankie packed her things. Frankie ran to her door and went inside. She threw a few things in a pink Louis Vuitton overnight bag and jogged back out to the elevators. She could've cared less if she had forgotten anything. She was just ready to get out of there as quickly as possible. Reese held Frankie in her arms as the elevator descended.

By the time they made it to the station, Frankie's face had turned back to its original color and her eyes weren't red anymore. Anthony's partner was waiting for them in the lobby as they all walked in hand in hand. She greeted everyone and began to talk to Jackie.

"Now, Jackie, please know that they cannot see you. When they come out, they are going to be holding cards with numbers on them. All we need you to do is identify who it was that assaulted you by telling us the number that he is holding. Do you think you can do that?" Anthony's partner said to Jackie as she walked them into the room. Anthony was standing in the corner. Freddie was there too with hatred in his eye.

"Yes ma'am." Jackie was holding onto her big sister's hand and then looked over at Frankie. Frankie nodded her head as if to tell Jackie everything was okay.

Anthony's partner pressed a red intercom button and announced, "Send them in." The lights on the other side of the glass turned on and the door on the right opened. In walked seven men all holding white cards with large black numbers printed on them. Frankie was staring at Jackie as the men entered the room. Jackie tensed up when she saw Tae walk in.

"That's him! Number five!' Jackie pointed and then turned to bury her head in her sister's chest. Freddie went ballistic.

"It *was* Blake!" Reese said in a disappointed tone. Frankie looked up to see who this infamous man was. Holding number five was Dr. Gregory Blake Taylor.

Twenty-One

THE SUN WAS just about to set as it lit up the sky with the most beautiful colors. A cool breeze from the lake flowed through the cabin spontaneously and kissed Frankie on her body ever so gently. She closed her eyes and tried to hold back the tears. She was tired of crying. She was actually surprised that she had more tears left to cry. She never thought that she could be hurt that bad again and she vowed to never let another man get that close to her. *Never again.* Frankie began to build a solid wall around her heart and decided to give up on love. She wished that she was able to turn back the hands of time and go back to the minute before she told Anthony she couldn't be with him any more. She would probably be enjoying that sunset with him at that moment.

Reese came walking up the yard from the pond. She was wrapping a towel around her soaking body. Reese could swim like a fish and jumped in the water whenever she could. She shook the water out of her hair and splashed Frankie.

"Reese, grow up." Frankie said jokingly as she wiped her face. Reese flicked her and walked inside to the bathroom. Frankie heard the shower running and then heard Reese's voice. She was singing. Frankie loved to hear Reese sing. That was a talent that no one knew she had. Frankie had spent years trying to encourage Reese to sing out in public but Reese never thought her voice was good enough. So she stuck to singing in the shower.

Summertime...
And the living
Is easy...
Fish are...jumpin'
And the cotton....
Is high...

Frankie sat back and hummed along as Reese continued to sing.

Your daddy's rich...
And you ma is...
Good lookin'...
So hush...
Little baby
Don't you cry.
So hush, little baby
Don't you cry...

Reese continued to sing that song a couple more times and then she turned off the shower. She rubbed the mirror to reveal her own face. She looked at herself and she smiled. She was loving who she was regardless of whether the men in her world thought her to be worth love or not. She knew she was worth it. She just had to make herself believe it. She began to sing another tune.

You are beautiful
No matter what they say...

"Hey Frankie! You beautiful girl!" Reese hollered form the bathroom and laughed.

"You too sista!" Frankie responded. She laughed to herself because she knew what song was coming next.

Sista!
Remember yo' name...
Oh! Sista!
Remember them niggas is lame!
Oh! Sista!
I'm keeping my eye on you!

Frankie burst out laughing. "Now you KNOW them ain't the words chick!"

"So shake YO SHIMMIES!!!! Woooo!" Reese was shouting, singing, and dancing for the next hour. She had Frankie up and dancing along with her. There wasn't any music playing except the music that was made between the pitter patter of their bare feet on those wood cabin floors, their laughter, and their love for each other.

Exhausted from dancing, the two best friends ended up on the hammock overlooking the lake. Swinging in the hammock with their bare feet hanging off the edge, they both closed their eyes. It wasn't often that they took the time to rejuvenate like this. It wasn't like they couldn't. They both had pretty lenient careers. They just never took the chances that they had. They were always working and looking for love in the wrong places.

"Reese?" Frankie mumbled in a relaxed tone.

"Yeah?"

"Why won't you go public?" Frankie asked.

Reese didn't know what she meant. "Public?"

"With your singing?"

Reese huffed. "Frankie, you know how I feel about that. Why you keep pressing the issue?"

"Cause I really think you have a beautiful voice. I wouldn't tell you that if it wasn't true." Reese didn't respond but she took Frankie's suggestion into consideration. They continued to swing back and forth as the sun began to set holding hands. The two best friends fell asleep under the moonlight. On the hammock.

Twenty-Two

WORK HAD GOTTEN so hectic to the point that when Reese called and suggested they go out for drinks, Frankie had to take her up on the offer. Frankie was hesitant though.

"Reese, I don't know. You know how you get." Frankie said in a motherly type tone.

"Frankie, I promise. Just drinks and then we go home. Pinky swear! I know you got an image to uphold. Shoot, I do too these days. I haven't been out with you in a while and wanted to hang for a bit." Reese whined.

"Aight…Reese I ain't playing with you!" Frankie warned.

"Yeah, whateva…I'll be at your house by time you get there. Love you."

"Love you too."

Usually Frankie would turn Reese down because whenever they went out together, Frankie would usually end up having to break up a fight and she sure didn't feel like doing that every Friday or Saturday night.

Reese was a spit-fire and proud of it. She claimed it was her Hispanic heritage that caused her to act like that but Frankie would always correct her. "Don't even go there Reese, it's the ghetto in you that make you act like that." She would roll her eyes and promise that she was getting better, but Frankie had yet to see any significant change, although she had to admit, Reese had toned it down a bit.

Music could be heard from her penthouse as she stepped off the elevator and her floor of her building complex. "I swear! Reese is going to get my put out." She mumbled to herself. She turned down the hallway and before she could get her key in the lock good, Kenny, from across the hall, and his lover Mark swung their door open so quickly that it made Frankie jump.

"Gur-friend! You needs to get that foolishness under control...ah-kay?" Kenny pointed to her door as he placed his hands on his hips. Kenny and Mark were both wrapped in pink velour and satin housecoats and wearing slippers. Mark just curled up his lips and raised one eye-brow as if to co-sign for Kenny. "We have been working hard all week and don't wanna hear none of that Jizzle fo' shizzle. We are trying to relax. Ah-kay?" Kenny and Mark both snapped their fingers in unison.

"I apologize guys. I have guests and they don't know the rules. As soon as I get in there you won't hear a sound. I promise. Have a good night."

"Umm-hmmm." They both sung in unison and went back inside.

Frankie turned the lock and was not surprised to see Reese dancing around in nothing but her panties. When she saw Frankie, she immediately grabbed an outfit that was lying on the edge of the peanut-butter-colored leather couch. She pointed to the outfit while shaking her hips. Frankie pointed to her ears and walked over to the coffee table, grabbed the remote and turned the music down.

"So?" Reese asked as she downed a glass of red wine, still dancing to the music.

"So, what?" Frankie responded as she laid her briefcase and keys down and slipped her heels off. She sat down on the couch and rubbed her burning feet.

"Uh…the outfit chick. What do you think?"

"Yeah."

"Yeah what? You likes?" as she started dancing like a stripper with the outfit dangling in front of her half naked body.

"It's cute Reese." Frankie wanted a drink and wanted to go out, but she was really exhausted.

"Glad you like it…cause this is what you're wearing." Reese threw the outfit on Frankie's lap.

"Oh, no ma'am…You are not about to dress me tonight." Frankie picked the outfit up and placed it back on the arm of the couch.

"Why not? Girl you be trying to wear your work clothes and there is no way you are going to get a man like that!"

"Who said I wanted one?"

"You need one wit'cho lonely self! I'm tired of watching movies every night with you! Besides, it's been almost a year since Greg…better known as Blake…better known as Tae." They laughed. It was so much easier for them to laugh at the situation these days, but admitted there was nothing funny about the issue.

"Whateva hussy!" Frankie snatched the outfit and walked off to the bathroom to get ready. She took a quick shower, dressed, and out the door they went.

Twenty-Three

THE WIND CAUSED the sheer curtains to flutter as he lifted up the window. It was a cool night, and Thomas felt like letting in a little of the breeze. He stretched out on the couch and continued to flick through the channels. There was never anything good to watch on Friday nights— which was usually why he was always at work or in the streets. Normally, during this time, he was usually still at work or having a few drinks with Julian and Vincent, his two best friends and line brothers.

His hip vibrated. It was Vincent. "What it do, dawg?" Vincent hollered. There was loud music in the background.

"Aye man. Sup wit'cha?" Thomas fixed his eyes on the television screen which was now on a commercial for male enhancement pills.

"Yo, I'm up here at Street Lights with Juju. You comin' out?" Julian yelled an obscene greeting from the background. Vincent snickered. Thomas shook his head.

"Naw man. I'm jive tired, son." Thomas switched positions on the couch and changed the channel again. He placed his hand inside his pants.

"Dawg! Man it's bumpin' tonight dawg. And the honeys are out tonight—hey hotness!" Vincent shouted out to a woman walking past him at the moment. She must have ignored him based on his next response. "You ain't *that* fine no damn way trick!" Thomas laughed at his best friend's game or lack thereof. They were always causing women to either splash a drink in their faces or curse them out. Thomas got a kick out of watching them make idiots of themselves. He would then inform them to watch as he made his move. "So when you gon' get here man?" Thomas really didn't feel like getting up, but there wasn't anything else to do, so he figured he would go on and go.

"I'll be there in an hour man." Thomas hung up the phone and sat up. His phone rang again. It was Tonya. He did not feel like talking to her tonight but he figured that if he didn't answer then she would keep calling and clog up his voicemail box. "Hello." He tried to sound sleep.

"Hey baby. You sleep?"

"Yeah. What's up?" Thomas pumped out a fake yawn and stretched.

She sighed. "Oh nothin'. I was just calling to check on you. I hadn't heard from you in a while so I figured—"

"Been busy." Thomas tried to be as nonchalant with her as he could to get her to finally leave him alone, but it never worked.

"Ok…well are you busy tonight? I could use some Tom-tom, if you know what I mean." She changed her voice.

"Yeah Tonya. I'm busy tonight. Got family comin' in. As a matter of fact, that's them calling me now on the other line. I'ma have to call you back later."

She sounded disappointed. "Look Thomas, I'm sorry okay. How many times do I need to tell you? Please forgive me? I'm so—"

"Tonya. Let it go man! I told you already."

"Thomas, please." She begged, near tears. Thomas loved to hear her beg. He didn't respond. "Call me later?" She pleaded.

"Aight." Thomas hung up.

He hopped up and jumped in the shower. The hot water pounding on his face felt so good. He just stood there with both hands pressed up against the shower wall and tried to think of absolutely nothing. But that task was close to impossible. With as much as he had on his mind, there was no way he could *not* think about how pissed off he was with Tonya and how badly she had hurt him. But he *did* love the extra groveling she was doing lately. He wondered how long it would be before she stopped. He hoped it would last a little longer.

He stayed in the shower completely statue-like for the next fifteen minutes in a daze, thinking back to the day that started it all. He and Tonya had been dating seriously for the past three years and were even living together. It had been two hours since she had left, and Thomas was getting antsy. He suspected that something might be wrong so he called her cell phone. No answer. He pressed re-dial. Again, no answer. He slammed the phone shut and placed his hands behind his head. *Where the hell is she?* She had claimed that she was going to run to her mother's house real quick and then she was going to stop by the doctor's office to pick up her lab results. Thomas was anxious to hear the news. He stood up and paced back and forth, periodically looking out the window. *She should be here by now.* Thomas called her again.

"Hey this is Tonya. At the beep...make it do what it do baby!" *BEEP!*

Thomas refused to leave another message. He was pretty sure that she would notice that he had called over thirty times! He walked into the kitchen to grab a bite to eat. But he was so anxious that he didn't even have an appetite. He walked back into the living room and sat down on the couch. *Maybe a little television will keep me occupied until she gets here.* Thomas turned on the sixty-four inch plasma screen. At that moment, the front door opened. He jumped up to see a sad-faced Tonya.

"Baby! What is it?" Thomas ran to greet her.

"We're gonna have a baby!" Tonya screamed with delight.

"Awe girl! You got me!" Thomas picked her up and spun her around kissing her all over her face.

"Calm down Thomas! Don't hurt me!" Tonya laughed.

"Oh! My bad…my bad." Thomas placed her gently back on the ground and bent down to kiss her belly. He placed his ear up to her stomach and placed his left hand on her hip. "Sounds like boy to me!"

"Boy please, you silly." Tonya placed her hand on Thomas' head and smiled down at him. He stood up and kissed her again. He seemed more excited about the baby than Tonya did.

Thomas went out the very next day and spent over $5,000 on baby stuff. Tonya told him that was absolutely outrageous, but he insisted.

"Baby, for years I had to live without and now that I have the money to be able to do this, I'll be damned if my child is not going to lay his head on designer sheets." Tonya couldn't convince him otherwise, so she just sat back and allowed him to do it.

He filled the extra room with all sorts of diapers, and blankets, toys, a crib, a bed, a rocking chair, and tons of more items. The room was a sea of pastel greens and yellows. He figured that a girl or a boy could wear either color.

Thomas made sure that he put in more hours at the company to ensure that when the baby arrived, he would be able to leave the business in his Vice President's hands comfortably. The week that the baby was due, Thomas had to fly out to L.A. to wrap up some things with a client of his. He didn't expect the meeting to last as long as it did and while he was there, Tonya went into labor. Thomas ended his meeting abruptly and booked the next flight home. Due to weather issues, his flight was delayed and he missed the birth. Crushed, he called Tonya to speak with her and see how she was doing. She sounded tired.

"I'm good. He's doing really good Thomas."

"He? He? It's a boy! I knew it would be a boy!" Thomas hung up the phone and ran through the airport screaming, "It's a boy! I got a boy!" People all around him smiled and clapped as he did his famous touch-down dance.

Meanwhile, back at the hospital, Tonya wasn't the least bit upset that he wasn't there. Little did he know that she needed that time without him around to have the doctors perform the DNA test. By the time Thomas had made it back to D.C., Tonya had already been discharged and sent home. Tonya sat on the couch as she breastfed the helpless infant. Her cell phone rang. The baby didn't budge. Tonya smiled at the little life in her arms and answered her phone.

"Tonya, I need to know if he's mine or not." James fussed. Tonya heard a car pull up in the driveway.

"James, I will tell you as soon as I find out. I gotta go!" She whispered and hung up the phone as Thomas walked in the front door carrying a bouquet of roses.

"Hey babe! Who was that?" Thomas leaned over and kissed Tonya and the new baby on the head as he pointed to the phone.

"Oh…" hesitating, "That was Mama. Checking on the baby." She lied so easily, it was like second nature to her.

"Oh…well how's my boy doing?" Thomas took the baby from Tonya and began to rock him in the recliner. Tonya's phone rang and she got up to take the call in the bathroom. Thomas was so engulfed in the baby that he didn't even notice her leave the room. Within seconds, Tonya was grabbing her keys and purse and heading for the door.

"Babe, I'll be right back. My sister's got something she wants me to pick up for the baby."

"Why can't she bring it over here? You really need to be resting baby." Thomas stated without looking up.

"She can't leave the kids home alone, they sleep and Rick ain't home yet from work. Love you. I'll be back in a min." Tonya opened the door and sped out the driveway and down the street to the clinic to hear the results.

The nurse called Tonya to the back of the office after she had signed in and sat in the waiting room, impatiently. The nurse led her to a room in the back and asked her to wait there for the doctor. Tonya sat in the cold room as she waiting for the doctor to show up. James was blowing her phone up.

"Dammit James, I'm at the doctor's office now! I'll call you back!" Tonya slammed the phone down. She could not believe that she had allowed herself to fall into this predicament. All over sex. Her life could be ruined all because she wanted more sex. *How stupid? And of all people, why did I sleep with James?*

The doctor entered the room. "Tonya Phillips?"

"Yes. I'm Tonya." Tonya looked up, praying that he would tell her what she wanted to hear.

"Well I have the results here." He began to open the file. *Just tell me already!*

"Okay." Tonya was trying to be patient.

"Well, *you* are the mother..." He looked at her waiting for her to laugh. Her face was blank. "I'm sorry, a little doctor humor." The doctor cleared his throat and continued reading the report. "With a percentage of 99.99% James Reid, *is* the father." Tears filled Tonya's eyes as her heart sank. *Shit!* Was all she could think to herself. She stood up and thanked the doctor. She walked slowly back to her car as she tried to think of how she was or was *not* going to tell Thomas.

She opened the car door and was startled by James's presence behind her. "James you scared me!"

"Well. Am I the father Tonya?" James stared at her, looking for answers in her eyes. The tears told it all. Tonya felt a huge lump form in her throat. "Dammit Tonya, answer me!" he yelled.

"Yes James! Yes! You're the father okay!" Tonya climbed in the car and slammed the door. She backed out of the driveway and drove straight to her mother's house.

James stood in the parking lot with his head down. He didn't know whether to be excited that he was the father of that beautiful baby boy or should he be beating himself over the head for sleeping with his brother's fiancée? The pain of it all was still so fresh.

The hot water in the shower had now turned cool and caused Thomas to break away from his thoughts. He turned the shower off and reached his hand outside the curtain in search for his towel. When he felt someone hand one to him, he opened his eyes immediately to find Tonya standing there, in the nude. Seeing her standing there, naked, didn't bring a rise to Thomas' manhood, it brought back memories. Bad memories. All he could think of was how *his* brother, *his* flesh and blood, had sex over and over with her right up under his nose. In *his* home! Normally, Tonya's naked body made Thomas nutty, but ever since that day his brother confessed to him that that beautiful little boy was not his son and was actually his nephew, Thomas was never able to look at her the same.

He had given her everything. He had given her his all and she just threw it away. Her excuse was that he was always working, and his comeback was that she sure didn't have a problem shopping on his tab.

"Tonya, put your clothes back on, please." Thomas turned his attention from her to his reflection in the mirror. She continued to stand there. "Tonya, I'm not going to say it again. I need you to put your clothes on and get out."

"But baby, I realized...I messed up. I know I was wrong." She got down on her knees and attempted to please him orally. He pushed her head away and stepped around her.

Tonya knew that she had completely thrown a good thing away. He was a hard worker, he was successful, he was sexy, he was loyal...all in all Thomas was a good man. She followed Thomas to his room, steadily begging. Thomas enjoyed it while he was on the phone with her, but in person, he actually felt sorry for her.

"Don't you have *any* respect for yourself?" Thomas laughed at her as he got dressed. She didn't move. "Tonya! Get out!" Thomas screamed. He couldn't believe that she had gone this far and then he tried to think of how she got in his house in the first place. He had the locks changed. "How the hell did you get in here in the first place?" Thomas sat on the edge of the bed and put his chocolate colored gators on as he looked up at her.

"You left your door open." Tonya answered.

"Well then it should still be open. Get the hell out." Thomas stood up and tried to force her out. She didn't budge. Thomas got frustrated and began to curse and scream uncontrollably. Tonya became afraid and grabbed her things. She never wanted to get him to *that* point again. She threw on her jeans, t-shirt, and slipped on her flip flops and ran to the front door. She looked back to see Thomas coming straight for her. She put her hands in front of her face to block the blow. Thomas stopped before he got close enough. "Tonya, leave my house now. I never want to see you again!" He opened the door and pushed her out onto the front steps. Tears in her eyes, she looked at him and knew that he would never love her again, and she couldn't even be mad. He had every right.

Twenty-Four

BY THE TIME they got to the club, the line was wrapped all around the building. Reese had so many connections being *the* best female barber and the best stylist in all of D.C. period. With that clout, they pretty much walked up to the front and went straight to VIP. The DJ for the night had the room jumping, doing his thing and Frankie was in the mood to dance. She followed Reese to the bar. From the front door to the bar, she had been groped about five times.

"Men are such pigs!" Frankie hollered in Reese's ear. Reese just laughed and ordered two drinks for them.

"One cosmo and one apple martini both on the rocks!" Reese yelled over the music.

They each sat on the bar stools and danced in their seats. The place was packed and there was constantly someone that walked past every now and then that gave them something to either talk about or laugh at. The place was full of characters.

"Now what the hell was *she* thinking?" Reese leaned over and said to Frankie while pointing at a lady who was wearing a full cat suit covered in feathers. Frankie almost spit her drink out. Trying to control it and laugh at the same time, she managed to spill some on her lap.

"Damn! I'll be back Reese." She grabbed a napkin and began to wipe her skirt as she headed for the nearest bathroom. Before she made it to the door, she was bumped by a man in passing. He placed both hands on her hips and apologized. She noticed how piercingly beautiful his eyes were and for a moment didn't realize that she was staring. She regained her focus and walked into the ladies room.

It was packed of course. There were women prepping themselves in the mirror and some waiting on stalls. There were paper towels all over the floor near the trashcan and the room didn't smell clean. This was one of the reasons why Frankie hated going to these clubs. The bathrooms always smelled like fifty years of dirty underwear in a steam pit—with the doors closed.

She managed to squeeze in between two ladies who were putting on their make-up and gossiping. One was wearing what must have been *the* largest hoop earrings in all of D.C. The other one was tall with the longest fire engine red weave Frankie had ever seen. Trying not to laugh, she grabbed a handful of paper towels and soaked the edge of them with hot water. She started patting her skirt while eavesdropping on the conversation going on around her.

"Girl, I can't believe he lied like that!" The one with the huge earrings said as she lined her lips.

"I know, right? Straight lied. But it's good baby, cause I put it *on* him like you wouldn't believe. I bet his wife don't do it like I do," the tall one said as she swerved her hips and laughed. It amazed Frankie how some women could sleep with another woman's man and be okay with it. To her, those type women where the scum of the earth, and she felt that

140

they all had it coming. She sometimes wished that she could be there to witness when it did happen.

Frankie got the stain out as much as she could. She threw the wet paper towels in the overflowing trash and pushed the door open.

On her way back to her seat, she spotted Yahira, her long time girlfriend from high school. She walked over and slapped Yahira on the butt. Yahira turned around with her hand in the air in slap mode. Her expression instantly changed when she realized who it was.

"Girl! You was bout to get slapped!" She leaned over and hugged Frankie. "Damn girl, how are you? It's been a long time! Who you here with? Reese?"

"I'm doing really good. Yeah, Reese is over there." Frankie pointed in Reese's direction and noticed that Reese had a weird expression on her face which was usually not a good sign. Then Frankie saw the lady in the feather cat suit walk up to Reese. Reese put her drink down and stood up.

"Damn! Lemme go get that heffa, she bout to fight. Call me girl!" Yahira shook her head and chuckled to herself. She knew Reese's track record.

Frankie walked up and Reese gave Frankie her I-didn't-start-it look.

"Not tonight Reese. I told you!" Frankie placed her hands on Reese's shoulders and forced her back away from the cat-bird lady.

"That's right. You better git'cho girl!" The cat-bird lady yelled as she walked away.

Reese stood up and attempted to go after the lady. Frankie grabbed her and leaned over to whisper in her ear. "This is exactly why I don't like going anywhere with you."

"My bad Frankie. She called me out my name and you know…"

"It's all good. Don't wanna hear it. I just want to chill okay?"

"I dig." Frankie grabbed her drink and started back to dancing in her chair. Frankie finished off her drink and turned around to place it back on the bar table as the bartender was handing her another drink. She waved her hand to let him know that she didn't want another drink. He then pointed to his left and told her that the gentlemen in the white shirt had sent the drink her way. The guy waved and Frankie waved back. It was the guy that bumped her as she was walking to the bathroom.

She turned around to show Reese the drink and twisted up her lips. Reese just smiled and winked. The guy got up and started walking towards her. Frankie immediately turned and asked the bartender to pour the drink out a quickly as possible and hand her the empty glass when he was done. He looked at her like she was crazy. "You never know what people's intentions are." She explained. The bartender nodded and poured the drink out. By time the man got to her, she was holding the empty cup up to her mouth as if she had drank the whole thing.

"Wow, Miss Lady, looks like you gets it in," he said smiling. He was tall, dark, and very handsome. He had bright, pretty, white teeth and Frankie figured he knew that he was fine. *I can't do pretty boys. They too much drama.*

"No, not really. I haven't been out in ages. Thank you for the drink, but I can handle it." She held out a ten dollar bill. He just smiled.

"No one said that you couldn't, gorgeous. Just wanted to buy you a drink." He pushed her hand away gently.

"Yeah, because you are expecting a payment in some other type of form later. Look, I just came here to spend time with my girl." Just then, Reese leaned over and pinched her. Frankie tried her hardest to not change the expression on her face although she wanted to punch Reese in the leg.

"Wow...I tell you, you twenty-first century women are something else. Hello, I'm Thomas," he said with the same smile on his face and his hand outstretched.

"Hi Thomas. I'm...not interested."

"Oh, but you will be my dear. I'll see you around." And he walked away.

"What in *the* hell is wrong with you Frankie?" Reese nudged her. "He was fine! And don't have no problem spending his money on you apparently!" She pointed to the empty martini glass.

"Girl, I ain't in the mood for some Rico Suave trying to get in my bed no matter *how* much money he got. I just wanna chill with the bestest friend a girl could have." Frankie kissed Reese on the cheek and laughed. "That's all. Straight chill mode tonight." Reese looked at her with a blank expression and finished off her drink. Frankie playfully nudged her and snickered.

"Well, I'm bout to go on the floor...you coming?" Reese let out a small belch and stood up. Frankie hoped up off her stool and followed her to the dance floor.

Frankie looked around the crowded room and saw the fine guy who had bought her a drink standing towards the entrance. They made brief eye contact, and he disappeared through the door. Frankie and Reese spent the rest of the night drinking martinis and dancing the night away.

Reese and Frankie could barely make it through the door of Frankie's penthouse. Reese had apparently had too many drinks, and Frankie's feet felt like they were bleeding. She pulled Reese along and fumbled with her keys until she was able to fling the door open. Just then, the elevator at the other end of the hall chimed and out stepped Kenny and Mark looking "fabulous."

"Uh-unn! Gur-friend! That is so tacky." Kenny said as he pranced faster down the hallway towards them. Mark had his lips twisted as normal, and his hand on his hips as usual.

Frankie didn't feel like talking so she just ignored them and drug Reese in, closed the door behind her and locked it. Throwing her keys and handbag on the floor next to the couch and kicking off her pumps, she then continued to drag Reese until they made it to the guest bedroom, otherwise known as Reese's bedroom. Frankie flung her on the bed and pulled her shoes off. Reese had managed to pull everything else off herself except her panties. She smiled her normal incoherent intoxicated smile and climbed under the covers. Within seconds, she was knocked out. Frankie walked out the room and thought to herself *I can honestly say that I had a great time and she really did handle herself like a lady tonight.* Despite the slight altercation with cat-bird lady, Frankie was proud of her.

Twenty-Five

THE OFFICE CALLED and needed Frankie to come in early and put out a small fire. Frankie decided to drive to work instead of taking the subway.

"Awww! C'mon! You jerk!" as Frankie honked her horn. She was trying to get to the office before things got worse. She loved her job with a passion, and some thought she may have loved it just a little too much. She was told that she was a workaholic at times and needed a vacation.

The light had turned green, but the Lexus in front of her wasn't paying attention and wasn't moving. She could tell that he was on a cell phone. She honked her horn again, and he stuck his middle finger up in the air through his sunroof. Livid at this point, Frankie swung her black BMW over to the left and proceeded to maneuver around him. She didn't check behind her as she pulled out, and then next thing she knew, her car was kissing the side of another. She had been hit.

She sat there in the seat for a moment trying to pull herself together when she heard a knock on the passenger side window. She was a little out of it and shocked. She looked up, and there stood the guy from the club, Thomas. *Just what I need! Great.* She climbed over the middle console and opened the door. The driver's side was crushed up against the other car which made it impossible for her to get out on her side. She climbed out of the car and almost hit the ground. She reached for the door handle to try and break her fall but she missed it. He reached out his hand and assisted her completely out the car.

"I'm fine!" Frankie snapped, and snatched her arm away.

"Lady, you are something else! You would have hit the ground had I not grabbed your arm! What's the deal with you?" Thomas yelled.

"I wouldn't be in this predicament had you gotten off your damn phone and went! The light was *green!* Now I'm really going to be late!"

"Hold up! I wasn't on no damn phone! You pulled out in front of me!" At that moment Frankie looked over to see the guy in the Lexus that had shot her the bird. She was mistaken.

Thomas walked off and proceeded to pull a cell phone out of his pocket. Frankie could hear him calling the police and explaining to them what had happened. He got back in the wrecked car and waited. For someone who had just wrecked his Mercedes, he was nice enough to make sure that Frankie was okay, and she began to feel guilty for snapping at him and accusing him of being at fault. She walked over to his car where he was sitting with his legs hanging out of the car. He was apparently texting someone. *Probably his wife*, she thought to herself. All the men that Frankie had ever encountered were always low-down enough to try to pull women knowing that they had wives at home.

Frankie cleared her throat and he looked up from his phone. "Please forgive me for my behavior back there. I'm just in a rush to get to work. I have—"

146

"It's all good ma'. I have gotten used to you women these days with the whole 'Independent Woman' syndrome. Trust me, it's cool. The police should be here any minute." He looked back down at his phone and continued to type. Frankie didn't know what else to say. She stood there not knowing whether to continue to stand there or walk away. After a few more awkward seconds, she chose to walk away and wait for the police. In the meantime, she made a quick phone call for a taxi cab, and to her office to walk Amber through the crisis that she was rushing for in the first place.

By the time the cab arrived, the police were finished gathering all the information they needed for their report. Frankie fumbled through her purse and pulled out a business card. When she looked up to find Thomas, he was standing right in front of her with his business card in hand as well.

Frankie smiled a fake smile and with her focus on the card said, "All my information is on there. I will make sure the insurance gets taken care of." She grabbed his and he took hers with the most gorgeous smile. It was the same smile she saw that night at the club.

"Thank you. I'll hold you to it. Aye, it was really good to see you again," he paused and looked at her business card, "Frankie? Too bad it was under *these* circumstances." He winked and walked off.

When the rental car arrived, he looked back and waved at Frankie as she climbed into her cab.

"It was good to see you too," she called out at the last minute, and he nodded his head. He sure was fine, and Frankie sure was interested. Just as he said she would be. As soon as she got to work she called her insurance company. Once she got everything lined up, she decided to give Thomas a courtesy call to update him on the progress she had made. She reached into her purse and pulled out the card that he had given her. She dialed the number. As the phone rang, she reached up and grabbed a lock of her long black hair and twirled it around her index finger.

"Thomas Reid," the voice on the other end said.

"Hi Thomas, this is Frankie. Frankie Leone."

"Oh, yes. How could I forget? The gorgeous woman who plowed me and blamed me for it. Nice to hear your voice," he said jokingly.

Sounding irritated Frankie tried to inform him of why she was calling. "Well I was calling to—"

"Well the answer is yes," he interrupted.

"Yes? Yes to what?" Sounding confused now, Frankie stopped playing in her hair and sat straight up.

"Yes, I will go to dinner with you. I mean, I hate to hear a woman beg," he laughed. Frankie rolled her eyes.

"Anyways! What I was calling you for was to let you know that I have gotten the insurance taken care of. They should be contacting your company soon."

"Oh…great. Now what time are we going to dinner?"

"Who said I was going to dinner with your Mr. Reid?" Frankie sounded aggravated but deep inside she liked his sense of humor.

"It's the least you can do for an innocent man who was simply trying to get to work. You almost killed me woman!" he changed his voice to sound like he was crying. Frankie smiled and he could tell it in her voice. He smiled and gave himself a pat on the back for overcoming a small hurdle with this tough cookie.

"Well I guess dinner won't hurt." She gave in.

"Hell, it shouldn't. Getting hit by you is what hurts. I'll pick you up at six."

"But you don't know where I live."

"I don't need to know where you live. I have your work address right here on the card you gave me. I figured that you got off around that time," he explained. Frankie agreed to six o'clock and hung up the phone. *He's good.*

She finished up as much work as she could by six. At a quarter to, she shut down all the computers, turned out all the lights, set the alarm, walked outside, and looked around the parking lot. There Thomas was, waiting patiently with the engine running. He was punctual—a favorite trait of hers. She hated being late to anything. *One point for Thomas.*

"How was your day?" he asked as she stepped in the car.

"Fine. Busy of course." She replied as she looked out the window. He nodded his head as if he had expected her to say that.

Frankie didn't ask where he was taking her. He seemed like a take charge type guy and she assumed he had already selected a place. Her assumptions were right. He had also picked one of her favorite places, Le Bourgeois. It was an upscale lounge that she loved to dine in. The food and the service were worth the high-end prices. It was always hard for her to get Reese to go with her, so she very rarely went. She would always have to offer to pay to get Reese to go with her. Reese claimed that all the "sadiddy" black folk went there. "And I can't stand no saddidy folk," she would say.

"Is this fine?" He put the car in park and turned to Frankie, awaiting a response. Frankie looked at him and there was that smile again. *Man, his teeth are so white, and his lips...wow.* Frankie tried her best not to smile.

"Uh, yes. This is one of my favorite places actually. You chose well." She grabbed her purse and reached for the door. Thomas placed his hand on her arm. Frankie pulled back and looked at him like he had just slapped her.

"Whoa…hold up a sec!" Laughing to himself, Thomas jumped out the car and ran around to her side and opened the door for her. *A little much over the top* was what she was thinking to herself, but nevertheless, she stepped out and thanked him. *I guess men do that, thinking that it's earning them coochie points.* She thought again to herself. Ever since Greg, whenever men did things like that for Frankie, she always discounted their efforts and couldn't have cared less if another man ever did it again.

The hostess showed them to their seats and handed them two menus. Thomas raised his hand and told her that they would not need any menus and that he was ready to order their food. Frankie looked at him again like he had just slapped her.

Looking at Thomas with one eyebrow raised Frankie said, "I'm sorry, ma'am, I'm not ready to order. I would like to take a look at the menu." Thomas tried to not allow the fact that he was irritated to show on his face. He then reminded himself that he didn't really know her like that to be trying to order for her in the first place. The hostess grinned and handed Frankie the menu.

"Your server is Tina, and she will be with you shortly. You two enjoy your meal." The hostess returned to her podium.

"You just don't give in do you?" Thomas said with a smile on his chocolate face, speaking softly with his head lowered closer to the table.

"Has nothing to do with giving in, sweetie. Has everything to do with you not knowing me well enough to order for me." Frankie picked up the menu and began to search for her usual.

"Well let me try something…" Thomas looked at her as she raised her eyebrow again and twisted up her lips. Thomas reassured her.

"Nothing fresh ma. I just wanna play a little guessing game." She lowered her guard. "Let me guess what you *would* order."

Frankie grinned and got sarcastic with him. "You do well at selecting the restaurant so now you think you can tell what entrée I would order? Have at it. Humor me." She continued to look through the menu.

"Hmmmm...lady like you...let's see. You're not an Alfredo girl, so the Fettuccine Alfredo is out." He looked at her as if she was going to give him a signal of whether or not he was on the right track. Frankie ignored his silent request and continued to look at the menu. While he was still sizing her up, she found what she had planned on ordering, placed her index finger on it and looked up at him. He continued with his analysis, "You look more like a chicken kinda girl...so I am going to take a stab at it and say that you would be more apt to order the Chicken Pont alba with the Béarnaise Sauce on the side. I say on the side because you seem like a neat freak and wouldn't like the sauce all over your food, you'd rather dip." He paused. "Yeah, you're a dipper." Confident in his diagnostic evaluation, he leaned back in his chair and folded his arms, waiting for a response from Frankie.

"Actually, Alfredo isn't that bad." She lied. Frankie absolutely hated Alfredo sauce. "And I was looking more along the lines of the Shrimp Etouffee, but nice try." She patronized him and giggled in a you-think-you-know-but-you-have-no-idea type way, then removed her finger from the Chicken Pont alba with Béarnaise Sauce item on the list and decided to order the Shrimp Etouffee instead. *Man, he was good!*

Twenty-Six

IT HAD BEEN a long time since Frankie had seen Ms. Robin, Reese's mother. Ms. Robin was like a second mother to Frankie. As a child, growing up, whenever Frankie couldn't talk to her own mother about certain issues, she would talk to Ms. Robin. When she decided that she was ready to have sex with Anthony, she talked to Ms. Robin about it. Ms. Robin made her change her mind, temporarily. She had convinced her to wait and save herself for *the one*.

Ms. Robin was respected throughout the whole neighborhood. She was the "cool mom" and she always spoke words of wisdom. Although Frankie respected what Ms. Robin always had to say, she disregarded her speech on abstinence and made the decision to sleep with Anthony later on down the line. She regretted it, of course.

Frankie and Reese had pulled up to the yellow row house at about a quarter to nine. There was one light on in the front room which meant that Ms. Robin was up reading her Bible. They stepped out of the car, and Frankie started swatting mosquitoes as Reese was slapping gnats out of her face. They both knew that they would be itching and scratching by the time they made it inside.

Desperately Devoted

They approached the front door where Uncle Pete was sitting on the porch smoking a cigar and coughing. Frankie just shook her head, and Reese called out to him. "Uncle Pete...you ain't dead yet?" Frankie smacked Reese on the arm. "What?" She turned to Frankie. "He keep suckin' them cancer sticks! And you hear him hacking up his lungs."

Uncle Pete looked up. "Aw, hursh chile! Watch how you speak to grown folks." And he continued to cough. Reese walked over and kissed him on the head.

"Hey, Uncle Pete." Frankie called out as she walked up the steps to the porch. Puddin' Pie, Ms. Robin's cat ran across Frankie's feet. "Dang, Puddin' Pie still here?" Frankie laughed. "Wow." They walked inside, and the screen door banged up against the door frame. Ms. Robin looked up from her reading.

"Hey mama!" Reese ran to greet and kiss her. Ms. Robin looked so happy to see her baby girl. She touched Reese on her face and just stared into her eyes.

"Lawreese Anna Mae...look at you." Frankie snickered and Reese tightened up. She absolutely hated her name although she *was* named after her father, Lawrence, she felt that her mother could have done a better job at the name. "You hongrey, baby?" Ms. Robin took her glasses off and laid her Bible down on the coffee table. She got up out of her rocking chair and then noticed Frankie standing there. "Is that Francesca Louise?" Reese snickered louder and Frankie just smiled.

"Yes ma'am. It's me." Frankie stood there like she was a child again.

"Ohhhh...look at you girls. She walked over to Frankie and placed her hands on Frankie's hips and shook them. "You had any babies yet with these baby makin' hips. You always *was* built like a brick house!

Hee...hee." She gave Frankie a kiss and hug. "Ya'll go on an' wash up. Mama gon' fix ya'll a plate."

"Yes ma'am." Frankie and Reese sounded off in unison. They walked to the back of the house and washed their hands. The bathroom was just as they remembered it growing up. There were copper plated butterflies hanging on the wall across from the cream colored toilet. The green wall paper with white daisies still covered the walls. The maroon shower curtain and matching towel and rug set had been replaced by a nave blue set.

On the way back to the kitchen they stopped in the living room to look at the pictures that were all over the walls. There were many of Reese and her siblings, and there were many of Reese and Frankie together as well. They walked up to their favorite one. Frankie was wearing the ugliest jumpsuit and Reese had on a pair of torn jeans and sneakers. They were sitting on the steps of the house, and Reese was brushing Frankie's long black hair. They both stood there and admired the photo. Both of them thought back to how simple life was then.

Ms. Robin's voice broke the silence. "Ya'll was inseparable. Couldn't pull ya'll apart...ya'll remember that day?" They nodded their heads and then looked at each other. They couldn't believe how fast time had flown. Walking back to the kitchen, Ms. Robin mumbled, "Time waits for no one."

Frankie and Reese followed her to the kitchen. They sat down as Ms. Robin placed hot plates of catfish and grits in front of them. Both of their eyes got big as golf balls.

"Oh no she didn't Reese! Ummm-mmm-mmm!" Frankie yelled out. Reese was laughing and Ms. Robin just smiled. That was their most favorite meal when they were growing up.

154

They finished eating and joking around and then ended up back in the front room with Ms. Robin. Reese was sitting on the floor between her mother's legs as Ms. Robin brushed her hair. Reese always felt safe in her mother's arms. Frankie lay on the couch next to them and watched. Just like old times.

Ms. Robin knew that this was an opportunity to speak something meaningful into their ears. She knew that they were in need of encouragement of some sort. She didn't know exactly what was going on, but because Reese was her child and Frankie was just like her own, she knew when her babies were in need of a good boost.

"Lemme tell you gals something." They both looked up at her. "You both been looking for that perfect kind of love. That love that's full of happiness. But you know good 'n well you been looking in the wrong places. And *you* Reese, just actin' all crazy, and not caring about other people feelings…"

"Mama, it's so hard out there to find love. So why should I be nice and *care* about them! It's just easier to be heartless." Reese tried to explain.

"No it ain't, baby. It's closer than you think. Besides the love of God, there is another kind of love that is just right. You have *got* to learn to love yourself. Once you do that, then everything else will be a walk in the park." Ms. Robin continued to brush Reese's hair.

"Ms. Robin…how do you get to that point? To that point where you love yourself so much that it don't matter who tries to hurt you…" Frankie was determined to figure out what she was talking about.

"I can't *explain* it to you babies. But I will say this…the day will come when you will know that you are there. You are going to look around, and you are going to understand what true happiness is. You are not going to know that you are on your way there *while* you are going through…until you arrive. And once you arrive, oh baby…it's the best feeling in the world." She stood up, and kissed them both on their heads. "Mama 'bout to go rest her bones now. Make sho' yo' Uncle Pete don't fall asleep out there. You know how he do."

"Yes ma'am." They both said in unison, and got up to go wake Uncle Pete. They could hear him snoring through the screen door.

Twenty-Seven

FRANKIE HAD NEVER played pool before, and was a little excited about going. Reese was tagging along because Thomas was bringing a friend of his as well. They walked into Fat Cats, and Thomas greeted them almost instantly.

"Hey, Frankie. Hey…" Thomas looked over at Reese.

"I'm Reese." She stuck out her hand. Then a slender light-skinned brother walked up, and cleared his throat.

"This is Julian. We call him Juju." Thomas placed his hand on the slender man's shoulder.

"Hello, ladies." Julian turned on his 'Barry White' voice, and Thomas laughed to himself.

"This way, ladies." Thomas led the way to the booth. The bar was full, and music was blaring as usual. Thomas sat next to Frankie, and Julian sat next to Reese. He put his arms around her. Reese looked at Frankie with her I-wish-a-brotha-*would* look, and Frankie kicked her under the table. She played off the pain, and gave Julian a fake smile. She knew already that she was in for a treat.

As they waited for their food, they decided to begin their pool game. Thomas showed Frankie how to hold the stick by leaning over her, but not intimidating her or pressing into her proximity. While on the other side, Julian was poking Reese with his own stick, and Reese had had enough.

"Nigga look, I don't need you all up 'n through here." Reese rubbed her butt in a huge circular motion.

"Nigga? Who the hell you callin' a nigga? Bitch." Julian's whole expression changed from Rico Suave to oh-hell-naw in zero point five seconds. Apparently, they were both hot headed, and were about to go to blows. Frankie knew that if she didn't make it over to Reese's side within a matter of seconds, somebody was going to jail, and it was probably going to be Reese.

Frankie ran to Reese's side, and Thomas grabbed Julian. Julian's caramel toned face was now berry red. He was pissed. Reese had already pulled her earrings off, and kicked off her heels.

"Naw Frankie, gimme my Vaseline!" Reese hollered as Frankie held her back. "Don't nobody call me a bitch!" Reese was becoming uncontrollable. The bartender at the counter walked closer to them. Thomas was trying to calm Julian down as Julian was screaming for Frankie to let Reese go.

"Let her go Frankie! Let that bitch go! She bad! She bad! She think she a dude anyway! Let her ass go!" Thomas tried to push Julian back away as he kept screaming. Frankie turned to Julian, and warned him to stop calling Reese out of her name. At that moment, Frankie felt Reese on her back. She then saw Julian's whole expression change again from

158

oh-hell-naw to oh-she-done-up-and-done-it! Reese had spit in his face. There was no more controlling Julian. He went ballistic, and started swinging. Thomas couldn't control him any longer. A few of his hits connected with Frankie's face, and she went to the floor. Reese saw that Frankie had been hit, and she became another person.

By the time the fight was broken up, the police had arrived. Anthony walked in, and saw Frankie on a bar stool with a bag of ice on her face. He walked over to her. "Damn Frankie, you out here raisin' hell?"

"Tony, no. You know me better than that." Frankie looked up at him, and rolled her eyes. Anthony looked around the room, and spotted two guys holding Reese down. Her hair was out of place, and she was still screaming. She didn't have a bump or bruise on her.

"Naw, Frankie ain't had nothing to do with it T-Bird! It was all me! I shut that bastard down!" Reese stood up. But the two men pushed her back down in the seat. Anthony turned his head to look to the other side of the bar room, and saw Julian hunched over in a chair tending to his wounds. *Daumn! Reese messed him up!*

Julian did not press charges, thanks to Frankie sweet-talking him out of it. Thomas drove Julian to the hospital to get the gash that Reese left on his forehead, stitched up.

The police cleared out, and Anthony stayed behind. He looked over at Frankie who was still holding the bag of ice to her face. He scooted closer to her.

"You okay, Key-Lime?" He grabbed the bag of ice from her, and began to pat it himself. No matter how many years had passed between them, he still loved her as he did the day their eyes connected in the school cafeteria.

"Yes, I'm fine." She grabbed the bag of ice back from him, and called for Reese to get up and come with her. She was livid, but in a way,

felt like she couldn't totally blame Reese. That was one thing that Reese
didn't tolerate, and that was being disrespected, and called out of her
name.

"Thanks, Tony. Reese, c'mon." Frankie touched Anthony on his
hand, and grabbed Reese's. They walked to the car, and Frankie opened
the passenger side door so Reese could get in. Reese got in, and turned on
the radio. She turned it up, and started dancing so hard in the seat that the
car was shaking. Franking took a deep breath, and turned to see Anthony
walking towards her.

"No problem, Key-Lime. Ya'll be safe now ya' hear!" He tilted
his hat, got into his patrol car, and drove off. Frankie laughed to herself.
She was so encompassed in her own thoughts that she didn't even realize
how loud the radio was, and how hard Reese was doing the cabbage patch.

The next few dates that Thomas and Frankie went on were strictly
the two of them. There was no way either of them were willing to risk
another wrestling match. Thomas joked with Frankie about her friends all
being wrestlers.

"I'd have to admit, she messed my dude up though." Frankie
would just laugh. Who needed a bodyguard when she had Reese around?

Thomas had decided that he would like to take Frankie to a new
club that had recently opened up. He figured he would try to move on
with this love life and give love a try once more. After Tonya, he didn't
believe that he would be able to love anyone the same, again. He felt
different. But he was really into Frankie, and enjoyed being with her. She
allowed him to be the man in the relationship—which was extremely
important to him. Slowly he began to allow his romantic side to re-
emerge.

"Would you like to go to the Jazz Tavern tonight? I hear they have great entertainment and the best daiquiris ever." Thomas asked, and Frankie agreed.

He picked her up that night, and they drove to the club. The club was impressive with its live band, accommodating a lady singing center stage. Frankie stopped to listen to the lady belt out a classic oldie, and imagined Reese standing up there in her place. Oh how she loved Reese's voice. But she was still unable to convince Reese to go public.

The dinner was delectable, and he was right—the daiquiris *were* amazing. Thomas continued to tell her how beautiful she looked and how much he enjoyed spending time with her. She realized that she was allowing herself to become friendlier with Thomas with each date. She didn't want to because she didn't want to get hurt again. She told herself continuously: *We are just friends. Just friends. Nothing serious. Don't let him get too close Frankie. Focus.*

After about six weeks, Thomas and Frankie were talking more often, and seeing more of each other as well. He was spending a lot of time at her place, and she at his. They were always on the phone if they weren't in each other's presence. Frankie tried her best to resist Thomas, but he was laying the gentleman behavior on thick. He was determined to prove to himself that he was over Tonya, and that he *could* love again. Frankie, at first, just assumed that he was being a gentleman just to get her in bed. So she figured that the longer she held out, he would eventually get tired of faking, and show his true side. After a few more weeks of his consistency, Frankie actually started to believe that this was who he really was. She also kept in the back of her mind that he *was* still a man. He would probably disappear the minute he got out of her bed. *Let's face it, that's what all men are after anyways. They only have one thing on their minds. He think he 'bout to hit it and quit it, but I got news for him...Ms. Robin ain't raise no fool!*

Twenty-Eight

THE DAY HAD BEEN a fairly hectic one, and Thomas had called a few times when Frankie was too busy to talk. Every time she picked up her phone and heard his voice on the other end, she continued to tell him to give her a call back in an hour or so, and he would. But every time he called back, she was still in the middle of something, and not able to really talk with him as he desired.

It was getting late, and everyone else had left for the day. Frankie still had a few more accounts that needed reconciling. She decided to finish the current one she was on, and then head home. The office was so quite that she could here a pin drop. Her phone rang, startling her.

"Frankie Leone."

"Hey, busy lady," Thomas responded.

"Hey, you. I have really been tied up today. It's calmed down a bit. What's up?" Frankie shuffled through a few papers on her desk.

"Well, I'm outside. Can I come in?"

"Oh…yeah I guess." Frankie was surprised. "I have just a little bit of work left to do though." She warned.

"No problem. I have something for you."

"Ok. I'll be right down." By the time she got to the front door, Thomas was standing there with a basket in his hands. The security guard buzzed him in after Frankie informed him that Thomas was with her. Thomas walked in, and Frankie greeted him, "What's this all about?" She pointed to the basket.

"Well, I figured that you have been tied up here all day, and I'm sure you haven't eaten dinner yet...so...here's dinner. You gotta eat eventually, right?" Thomas held up the basket. "I've been calling you all day to see if I could take you to dinner. And since I couldn't take you to dinner, subsequently, I figured I would bring dinner to you." He held the basket up in the air even higher, and patted the basket while grinning. Frankie led him upstairs to her floor. He followed her down the hall to the conference room where she had papers sprawled out all over the table.

"Looks like a train wreck in here, please excuse the mess. Business is really picking up," Frankie said as they walked into the room.

"That's a good problem to have. Here, let's eat right here." He pointed to the floor, laid the basket down, opened it up and pulled out a blanket. *Prepared.* Frankie was impressed but tried her best to not let it show.

She sat down on the blanket, and reached for the basket. He lightly popped her hand, "Excuse me, young lady, and please back up off my basket." Frankie smiled, placed her hands in her lap, and watched as he unpacked the basket onto the floor. He then pulled out three styrofoam containers. Steam was escaping from the sides. Just by looking at it, it was obvious the food was piping hot, whatever it was. By now, the smell of the food began to fill the air. Frankie perked up.

"Oh my goodness, is that Chief's Bar-b-que?" She exclaimed. Thomas just smiled, and began to open the cartons. "It is Chief's! Man! I haven't had Chief's in a minute!" Frankie was so hungry, and that Bar-b-que was certainly going to hit the spot. She was starting to wonder if he had somehow stumbled upon Reese, and was getting outside help. He was really peaking her interests more and more. But she couldn't let him in too much. Getting too involved right now would not be in the best interest of her career or her heart. She kept reminding herself to stay focused. *Stay focused Frankie!*

They ate and talked in between bites. Frankie was trying her hardest to not look like a pig, but for one, she was hungry and for two, Chief's wings were the best ever made!

"Uh...babe, you've got a lil'...somethin'...on your"—he was rubbing the side of his mouth. Frankie immediately rubbed her mouth but apparently didn't rub off whatever was on her face. Thomas moved closer to her, and with a napkin, wiped her mouth ever so softly. They sat there, eyes locked on each other, and before either of them knew it, they were kissing.

One peck.

Then two.

Then steady. Frankie was trying so hard to pull away, but her lips wouldn't let her. Then she felt his hand slide up her left arm, and then rest on her breast. She immediately stopped the kissing, grabbed him by the wrist, twisted it, and looked him dead in the eye. "It's time for you to go now, Thomas. I have to get back to work."

"I didn't mean to..." Thomas said sounding remorseful.

"It's okay." Frankie said reassuringly. "Really though, I think you should be going." Frankie began to help him clean up the dinner plates and utensils.

"Call you tomorrow?" he asked hopefully. Frankie nodded and walked him outside. As he drove off, she politely waved, and then skipped all the way back to her office with a school girl smile on her face.

Twenty-Nine

FRANKIE WAS A LITTLE excited about her mother meeting Thomas. They had been seeing each other for close to a year now. And she thought that she would never be able to allow another man into her life like she had allowed Greg. She began to feel that Thomas was genuine, and had finally decided to lower her guard just a little, and let him treat her like the queen that she had begun to believe she was. Thomas was the most persistent man that she had ever met. She had become successful at scaring away all the other losers, but for some reason, he was determined to stay around, and he hadn't even *touched* the goodies.

Thomas was romantic and thoughtful. He was intelligent and sexy—which was always a plus in her book. He wasn't like all the other pretty boys that she had met. He wasn't like them at all. If he was, he was a great actor.

There were many things that Thomas had done to show her that he was willing to give his all. From having the local radio station call Frankie at work and have him over the air tell America how wonderful a woman she was, to showing up at her job in a clown suit to deliver a singing telegram about how much she meant to him. Yes, his friends called him corny, but he knew that things like that were unique and that she would remember his corny antics over a lame dinner and movies bit any day. But the pièce de résistance that won him a ticket to enter in through the huge wall that Frankie had spent so much time building, was the stunt he pulled on her thirtieth birthday.

Frankie had honestly planned a huge pity party and decided that she would work her way into thirty, but Thomas was adamant about that not happening—not on his watch. He had hooked up with Reese and they were in cahoots. He even had Frankie's co-workers in on it. That morning, she arrived at the office, within the first thirty minutes, there was a package delivered that was addressed to her. She opened it up and there was a red envelope tied with a black ribbon. She opened the envelope and inside was a gift card with $2,500 on it to Boutique de Janét, her favorite boutique! There was also an elegant handwritten note from Thomas that read: A LADY SUCH AS YOURSELF SHOULD BE TREATED LIKE THE QUEEN THAT YOU ARE. GO OUTSIDE.

Frankie walked briskly down the corridor and out to the parking lot. There was Thomas, dressed in a tuxedo, standing in front of a stretch limo. On the windows, there was screen printing that read: HAPPY BIRTHDAY, FRANKIE LEONE.

Frankie walked over to Thomas and gave him a hug and kiss, "Tommy, what's all this, baby?"

"Well I want you to celebrate turning thirty, in style. You deserve it. I love you Frankie." A huge knot formed in her throat. *Love? Love? Oh no...*her lips were trying their hardest to prevent the words from coming out of her mouth.

"I love you too, Tommy," the lips lost. This was the first time that those words had been exchanged between them, and they both knew it. And as terrified as they both were of those three words, it didn't hurt as badly as they thought it would when they spoke them.

"Go get your things, baby. I will be waiting right here. Today is your day." Frankie didn't argue about all the work that she needed to do. She just ran back inside and grabbed her purse. Mike, Patrice, and a few other co-workers were in the lobby just grinning from ear to ear. She pointed at them jokingly, grabbed her things and left out.

Thomas opened the door for her, and she stepped inside. The first stop was Chantal's Salon. Frankie got her hair done, eyebrows waxed, facial, manicure and pedicure. Once she was done there, she was driven to Boutique de Janét and went absolutely crazy. She bought shoes, and hats, jewelry and clothes. Frankie was in heaven. Thomas just sat back and watched it all go down with a smile on his face the whole time. Seeing her that happy made him happy.

The next stop was Frankie's house. She thought that this was the end of the road so she leaned over, planted a huge kiss on his lips, and thanked him.

"Oh…it's not over baby. Go upstairs. I will be right here waiting for you." There was more? *Oh my goodness.* She got on the elevator and tapped her foot impatiently as the numbers lit up. Her floor never seemed this far until today.

The doors opened and she ran down the hall to her door. There was a pile of red rose petals on the welcome mat. Frankie giggled like a little girl and fumbled for her keys. She opened the door, and her breath was taken away. Her living room was showered in red roses. There had to be over two-hundred dozen! There was another hand written note from

Thomas in the middle of the floor. It read: GO TO YOUR ROOM! YOU'VE BEEN A BAD BIRTHDAY GIRL! XOXO.

Frankie laughed, dropped all her bags, and ran to her room. On her bed lay *the* most gorgeous red gown and stilettos she had ever seen in her life. They looked just like the Kena J designer gown and shoes that she was eyeing in the catalogue the other day. To her surprise, it *was* the gown and those *were* the shoes! That gown was on *sale* for $4300 the last time she saw it and the shoes were retailing at $450!

There was another note on the bed: PLEASE GET DRESSED AND COME BACK DOWN STAIRS…I'M GETTING BORED WAITING ON YOU. I KNOW THIS GOWN IS GOING TO LOOK GORGEOUS ON YOU. XOXO.

Frankie went to the bathroom and took a shower. She had to shave her legs. She was so used to wearing dress pants that she rarely shaved. She made sure her make-up was still in tact from when she got it done at the salon. She double-checked herself in the hall mirror and admired her new gown. Not that she was unappreciative, but stylishly thinking, she was thinking that she needed a purse to go with the outfit, but nevertheless, it was still gorgeous!

She grabbed her purse and noticed another handbag on the stand by the door. There was another note: I KNOW YOU WERE THINKING THAT YOU NEEDED A PURSE TO GO WITH YOUR OUTFIT. HERE YOU GO…P.S. HURRY UP! XOXO.

She frantically switched purses laughing the whole time, and took off down the hallway to the elevator. If she weren't wearing those stilettos, she would have decided to take the stairs.

The doors to the elevator opened, and Frankie almost tripped trying to get through the lobby and out the doors. There was Thomas, still standing in front of the limo waiting for her. His eyes got huge when he laid them on Frankie.

"My…my…my you look absolutely gorgeous, Frankie. Just gorgeous!" He kissed her on the cheek, and opened the door to the limo.

"Well thank you, baby." Frankie said as she stepped inside the car. To her surprise, she was greeted by *all* her girls—Reese, of course, Patrice, Danielle, Yahira, Jai, Fie-fie, Zonya, and Sapphire. They were all dressed in black cocktail dressed and red stilettos. They all screamed, "HAPPY BIRTHDAY!!!" Tears filled Frankie's eyes. She pulled back out of the car and looked at Thomas. Before she could say anything he stopped her.

"Baby, I want you to have a girls' night out with your best friends. You haven't seen most of them in ages and I figured why not get them together for you."

"How did you? When did you?" Frankie was crying.

"While you were upstairs, I drove down the street to get them. They were waiting for me at Geno's Bar." He wiped the tears from her face. "Look, no more questions. The limo driver is prepared to take you *wherever* you wish to go. He is yours all night. Also, in the inside pocket of your new purse, which matches perfectly, I must say, is $3,000 for you to blow on you and your girls. Have fun, baby." Frankie tried to interrupt because she felt that this was just too much, but he wouldn't let her. "I love you and I want you to have a good time tonight. Go! Get in," he gently nudged her into the car. Frankie stopped, turned around and kissed him goodbye. He closed the door and waved goodbye as they drove off.

The entire night, her friends were gushing and talking on and on about how great of a guy they thought Thomas was.

"Girrrrrl! You done hit the jackpot!" Danielle said. All the other ladies agreed.

"I wouldn't say jackpot ladies," Frankie responded modestly. "He's just a sweet guy."

"Oh pa-leeze. Girl he got money *and* he romantic. No kids. No baby mama drama. Good job. And did I mention he got money?" Reese added. Everyone laughed.

"Oh just because he got a limo together does *not* mean that he got money," Frankie replied.

"Girl! He ain't just secure a limo for your bougie self! You see these dresses we wearing?" Yahira piped in. Frankie looked around the group and nodded with her eyebrows raised. "Well hell, you know I cain't afford no Kena J designer gown *and* heels."

"You mean to tell me, Thomas bought all ya'll these dresses?" They all nodded their heads as they patted their gowns in admiration. Frankie's mouth dropped. She sat back, and thought to herself, *maybe I did find THE one…finally.*

The jolt from the car being placed in park woke Frankie from her nap. Frankie knew her mother would just eat Thomas up once she met him but her father was a different story. No matter how great a guy Frankie thought he was, her father always found something. As long as he had money, her mother was sold.

Thomas turned the engine off. Frankie looked at Thomas.

"You nervous, babe?" She asked as she stroked his cheek.

"Naw girl. I'm a pro at winning dad's hearts."

"I won't even ask how many you have had to practice on." She smiled, and opened the door. Her father came running out wearing a stellar smile. He had just come back from golfing and was still wearing the sweater vest and plaid shorts.

"Pumpkin!" He called as Frankie ran to hug her father.

"Daddy. It's so good to see you." Frankie kissed him on the cheek. He grabbed Frankie, and tried to pick her up. Thomas was grinning from ear to ear. Her mother stepped out onto the porch looking as though she had just stepped out of a magazine. She too, was grinning, but looking at Thomas.

"Shelton put that girl down. She's just as big as you are." She stepped down off the porch and reached her hand out to greet Thomas. "How are you young man? Don't mind Shelton. I'm Vivian. You must be Thomas."

"Yes ma'am. Nice to meet you, Mrs. Leone." Thomas grabbed her hand and kissed it. Her mother oohed and blushed.

"Please...call me Vivian." It was obvious that she was loving that! Frankie's father grunted and reached out his hand.

"I'm Shelton Leone. You can call me Mr. Leone." Thomas shook his hand.

"Nice to meet you as well, Mr. Leone," Thomas smiled.

"Oh...I don't get a kiss on *my* hand? Is it like that, Thomas?" Shelton looked serious, but they all knew he was being a clown. And they burst out laughing.

"Daddy, leave him alone," Frankie snatched her father's hand and kissed him on the cheek again. Vivian just shook her head, turned, and walked back up to the house. Everyone followed.

Shelton and Thomas disappeared into the entertainment hall of the house to watch a football game that had come on while they waited for Maggie, their personal chef, to finish dinner. Frankie ended up in the living room with her mother. Her mother was propped up on a rose colored chaise lounge, posed as if someone was going to walk in any minute to take a picture of her. Frankie sat on the couch and closed her eyes.

"Sweetheart? Have you any idea when he is going to pop the question?" Her mother asked without moving from her picture perfect pose.

"No, Mother. I don't know."

"Well, I'm sure you are doing everything right." Frankie wasn't taken by surprise by her comment. It was just like her mother to think that there was a certain system to follow in order to get a man to do what you wanted him to do—especially when he had money. "I'm sure he will be asking you soon. And I've already decided on the location. I figured a nice elegant ceremony in Montego Bay. We could use sage and peach…don't you think that sounds darling?" *Unbelievable! She is always trying to control everything!*

"Sounds wonderful, Mother," Frankie sounded sarcastically enthusiastic. The two women sat there in silence until Maggie's voice over the intercom informed them that dinner was ready. They walked silently to the dinner hall, and sat at opposite ends of the large table. Thomas walked in behind Frankie's father, and had a slight grin on his face. Apparently, the time spent with her father went well.

Dinner was delicious as usual whenever Maggie cooked. Frankie loved Maggie's filet mignon and double-baked potatoes—which Frankie believed had been her best batch yet.

"Maggie…you did it again!" Frankie complemented as she dabbed her napkin to the corner of her mouth. Maggie smiled, and removed Frankie's plate. As a child, Frankie was a very picky eater. Maggie was the only one who was successful in getting her to eat just about anything.

Thomas seemed very comfortable with Frankie's parents. The conversation flowed smoothly, even during the times when Vivian would

174

try to veer towards the topic of marriage and children. Thomas handled everything very well. During a lengthy dialogue between Frankie's father and Thomas, Frankie learned that Thomas enjoyed playing golf. She knew that he was *interested*, and she recalled him watching Tiger play on television, but he never mentioned the desire to actually play until that evening. Thomas discussed the logistics of his information technology firm as Shelton picked Thomas' brain about a certain computer glitch he was dealing with on his personal laptop.

Frankie savored small portions of Maggie's delicious key lime pie as Thomas and her father exchanged their personal views on politics and gas prices. Frankie looked over at her mother who was nibbling on her food like a small bird would. Frankie rolled her eyes.

"Well, I'm telling you, if he *does* make it into office this year, I am most certain the gas prices will plummet," Thomas commented.

"You may be right, *but* the question is: will he make it that far? I'm not sure if America is ready for him." Shelton responded.

"Maybe America *isn't* ready…but I think it's definitely time for a change." Thomas replied with ease. He was definitely *not* intimidated by Frankie's father.

After everyone finished their dinner and enjoyed Maggie's rich and creamy key lime pie, they strolled out to the back patio to continue their conversation. Shelton and Thomas were primarily the ones controlling the conversation. Vivian would periodically pipe in and Frankie would only say something if she was asked a question.

Sitting on the back patio, listening to the crickets and watching the moon's light bounce off the pool, Frankie laid her head on Thomas' shoulder and closed her eyes as he, Vivian, and Shelton continued to talk. Before dozing off, Frankie heard Shelton and Thomas making plans to play a round of golf next weekend.

Thirty

SHE MUST HAVE forgotten to turn the heat on the night before because when she woke up she could see her own breath. Frankie shivered, and tried to block out the cold by wrapping herself up tighter in the huge down comforter. It didn't work. She turned over and looked at the clock. She still had a good two hours before she needed to get up.

"You aight, babe," Thomas moaned. Frankie looked over at him and pressed her hands under his chest. He flinched. "Girl your hands are too cold to be doing that!"

"Babe, I'm cold, can you go turn the heat up?" She whined. Thomas hated when she did that, but she would have kept aggravating him if he didn't. He flung the blanket off of his body and climbed out of the warm bed. Frankie rolled over into his spot and curled up in a ball as she waited for him to return.

Thomas crawled back in the bed on her side, and grabbed her in his arms. He pulled her close to his chest and held her as he drifted back off to sleep. He didn't want to let her go. He felt so good when he was

176

with her, and he knew that he loved her with every inch of his being. Tonya couldn't hold a torch to this woman.

The alarm went off and both Thomas and Frankie groaned loudly. Neither of them felt like moving. It was chilly and wet outside, and staying in bed was a more inviting option.

"Let's sleep in, boo." Thomas pleaded as Frankie tried to get out of bed. He pulled her in closer, and she kissed his forearm. He buried his head in her hair and smelt it. He loved the smell of her hair.

"Babe, we both got business to handle. You have a company to run, and I have clients to take care of." She closed her eyes as she savored his touch, and his body heat wrapped around her.

"I know…but you have been there long enough where they don't care what time you get there…and since I run my *own* business…I don't have to go in at all…which to me means we can sleep in. We never do it. What will one morning hurt?" He whined.

"Well…"

"Please." He squeezed her tighter from behind, and placed his lips near her lobe as he began to kiss her. She moaned. She wanted to stay in bed with Thomas all morning but she knew she had too much preparation for her next presentation this month.

After a few more soft and pleasurable kisses from Thomas' velvet coated lips, she gave in. The made love for the next hour and fell asleep in each others arms again.

Frankie woke up close to two hours later and climbed out of bed. She stood up and turned around to look at the gorgeous man lying in her bed who would soon be her husband in less than a year. She looked at the engagement ring on her finger and smiled. *Happiness…finally!*

Thomas had proposed to her a few months ago. He had invited her parents out to dinner, and had the waiter slip the ring in her wine glass.

He got down on one knee with tears in his eyes and Brian McKnight's "Let Me Love You" playing over the loud speakers. By the end of the proposal Frankie was in tears, and everyone in the restaurant was clapping, whistling, and cheering. Frankie's father looked at the couple approvingly and proud. He stood up to hug his future son-in-law and kiss his only daughter on the cheek.

"Congratulations, Pumpkin." He whispered in her ear. "Take care of my baby." He whispered in Thomas'.

"Welcome to the family dear," Vivian exclaimed as she hugged Thomas, "honey, stop crying, you'll ruin your make-up," she said as she hugged her daughter.

Frankie looked at the ring on her finger longer, and watched her future husband continue to sleep. She loved that man and he loved her. After standing there admiring him, she crept into the bathroom to get ready for work. She had a meeting with another one of the largest contractors in her region and was nervous. Thomas was her guinea pig and could probably recite her presentation word for word. He stayed up many nights listening to her and critiquing her on various aspects of her speech. Frankie knew that she was ready, but was still nervous. If she was able to accomplish this, her career would surely ascend to the next level tremendously, and she wouldn't have to work as hard or as late as she had been for the past three years. This account meant millions of residual dollars for Wallace NVest—which in turn was a lot of pressure on Frankie. With a huge success in this magnitude, Frankie would also be able to spend more time with Thomas—which was becoming an issue.

He had been understanding in the beginning, but lately he was more and more frustrated whenever he would call and she couldn't talk to him. Frankie was looking forward to having a little more time with him. She left him there, in bed, sleeping soundly.

Frankie's head was pounding by midday, and the work load kept coming. The files on her desk seemed to be multiplying by the minute and she hadn't had a lunch break yet—which, she figured, was probably why her head was hurting. She put her pen down and began to massage her temples. That temporary relief lasted only briefly before Amber came running in with more accounts to review. She pointed towards the growing pile of files that was lying on the floor next to the file cabinet. She had an assistant, but it seemed that she needed another one.

She stared at the piles of papers, the growing stack of files, her constantly expanding email inbox, and the ringing telephone, and she continued to rub her temples. It was as if there was a caller relentlessly pressing redial.

"Frankie Leone," she answered.

"Hey baby! I been calling," it was Thomas.

"It's been really busy today Thomas. Tara didn't come in today so we are short staffed."

"So I guess you are too busy to talk to me then, huh?" he was in defense mode. Frankie hated when he got like this. He wasn't like this in the early stages but had begun to act like this more and more frequently.

"Thomas, please honey. It's not like that, I promise. I love talking to you."

"Yeah, ok. Well when are you going to be getting off?"

"I'll be leaving here in just a few hours."

"A few hours, huh?" He paused. "Why don't you just come out and say it?"

"Say what, Thomas?" Frankie tried to keep her voice from sounding irritated but she was. And she was so ready to jump through that phone and strangle him. Her second line began to ring, "Thomas, my other line is—"

"Fine…you know what I'm talking about! Go ahead and answer your other lines! Go back to tending to your clients and taking care of everyone else but me! I guess I will see you when you decide to come home." Click. He hung up.

Frankie didn't even have the desire to deal with him at that moment. She had a deadline to meet and her prospective clients were on their way so she figured she would just deal with Thomas when she got home. She was sure he would be ready to discuss it sooner or later.

She finished her presentation and felt really good about how it was delivered. Frankie, Patrice and a few of her co-worker decided to stop by Geno's and grab a drink to celebrate. They also knew that if Frankie had landed *that* deal that they *all* would be getting paid more to compensate for the extra hours that they had been putting in. Frankie could honestly say that they were the best team to work with. She wouldn't have traded them for the world.

By the time she walked in the door, she knew she was going to hear it from Thomas. It was after nine, and Frankie admitted to herself that she honestly hadn't been giving Thomas the time he deserved. He was a great guy and all he wanted was to spend time with her. Was that so bad?

The lights were off and she could hear the television in the bedroom. She placed her briefcase and her keys down, and kicked off her heels.

"Wow…so you just come home whenever the hell you feel like it huh?" Frankie jumped because she didn't see him sitting in the dark, in the corner.

"No, Thomas. I was out having a celebratory type thing with the team from the office. I delivered a really great presentation." Frankie walked into the kitchen to look for something to eat.

"Oh, I see. You got time to go for drink, but when I simply call you, you're too busy. Or when *I* want to go out, you've got too much work to do. You know, Frankie that really hurts. After all that I do for you—"

"Thomas, baby, you know that I appreciate everything that you do for me." Frankie walked over to him, kneeled on the floor between his legs, and grabbed his hands. At first, she thought that she was seeing things, but then she looked closer and realized that he had been crying. "Baby, I didn't realize that I was making you feel like that." Frankie sounded very sympathetic. She began to rub his hands.

"Well you do." He looked away. Frankie stood up and pulled him up from his seat. She led him to the bedroom, turned off the television, and made pleasing him her main priority that night. They fell asleep in each other's arms—him with a smile on his face.

Those nights became more frequent. He would be feeling neglected and Frankie would be apologizing while giving him what he wanted—attention. It didn't always have to be sex, but he was willing to take that as well. His main need was simply attention, in any form. It got to a point where Frankie found herself continually checking in on him and reassuring him that she loved him and wanted him. He started becoming more sensitive, and more aggressive to the point that she was ready to end it. Frankie was not used to men openly showing emotion of this magnitude. She wasn't sure whether it was simply a result of how deeply Thomas felt about her, or if this was something that she really should have been concerned about. Regardless, engaged or not, she was tired. He was

181

draining her mentally and emotionally. Life was simpler when she was single!

Thirty-One

FRANKIE STEPPED OUT of the bedroom, and Thomas glared at her un-approvingly. "You're wearing that?" Thomas asked. They were on their way to a comedy show downtown.

"Uh, yeah…what's wrong with that I have on, Tommy?" Frankie looked at herself in the mirror, and twisted around to see her rear end—making sure that her panty line was not visible.

"You don't think it's a little revealing?" he asked. She was wearing a low cut Kena J blouse, and a pair of linen pants with her favorite high-heeled thong jeweled sandals. Her cleavage was showing a little, but she didn't see anything wrong with it. It was a classy outfit.

"I think it's very classy. I like it."

"Well bring a jacket," he stood up, walked up behind her, and looked at her through the mirror. "I just don't want anyone looking at *my* future wife." He wrapped his arms around her and kissed her on the cheek.

"Boy please, men are *gonna* look regardless, cause yo' girl is hot!" She bumped him with her hip and went to get her purse, "Let's go, you know you don't like to be late."

The entire ride to the club, Thomas kept looking at her out of the corner of his eye. Frankie turned completely to her right, and looked out the window the whole drive. As they stepped inside the club, a lady at the door checked their tickets. She then pointed them in the direction of their seats. Thomas stuck his hand out behind him, and Frankie grabbed it— allowing him to lead. He loved that she allowed him to be the man, and she knew how important that was to him, so she just did it to keep him happy. As they walked down the corridor, Thomas kept looking back at Frankie over his shoulder with a disturbed look on his face. He then clutched her hand tighter, and did his best to pull her in closer to him.

When they got to their seats, he leaned over and whispered in her ear. "You need to cover that up." He was starring at her chest with an irritated look on his face.

"Thomas, I'm fine." Frankie turned her head and faced the stage. She then felt his hand on her chin. He applied pressure to it, and turned her head to face him again.

"I didn't like those guys back there looking at you. I know you saw them looking."

"Thomas…not tonight!" She hissed. "Please, we came to have a good time. Can we do that?" He let her chin go and sucked his teeth. During the whole show, Frankie could feel his eyes on her the entire night. She tried her best to enjoy the show but if looks could have killed, she would have been dead. Once the show was over, Thomas grabbed her arm and led her to the car briskly.

"Tommy, let my arm go! You're hurting me! What is the problem?"

"You can't *tell* me that you didn't see that?" He pointed to a couple walking past. The couple slowed their pace down.

"Saw what Thomas?" Frankie folded her arms in defense.

"That nigga right there! You can't tell me you didn't see him looking all down your shirt!" By this time, the man Thomas had pointed out had stopped in his tracks. The lady he was with had begun to twist her face up. Thomas turned to him.

"Yo, son, I don't know who the hell you callin' nigga, but I ain't the one kid!" the man yelled as he stepped in closer to Thomas.

"I was *talking* 'bout you, *son!*" Thomas mocked the man. "All night you couldn't keep your eyes off my lady. That's straight up disrespect!" Thomas was face to face with the man now. Frankie backed away praying that Thomas wouldn't start fighting this complete stranger.

"I see you's a lil' sensitive 'bout yours son, but wasn't nobody eyeing your lady. You got the wrong one." The guy held up his hands, and walked back towards the lady he was walking with as she proceed to inform him that if he *had* in fact been looking at Frankie, she was going to stab him once they got home. She grabbed his hand, and dragged him down the street, fussing the whole way as she kept looking back at Frankie. Frankie walked around to the passenger side. Thomas came around to where she was, and opened the door for her. She stepped inside, and he slammed the door shut.

The drive home was a long and quiet one. Frankie was embarrassed, and enraged that Thomas had completely ruined the evening with his silly antics. Thomas was upset that Frankie hadn't worn a different shirt as he requested. Frankie really needed to talk with Reese but was never able to have a decent conversation with her because if

Thomas was anywhere nearby, he would swear that she was robbing him of quality time. It had been a while since she and Reese had hung out or talked for that matter. Reese had finally been able to open her own salon and Frankie hadn't even had the chance to celebrate with her. After running various scenarios through her mind, she figured out a way that she could get from up under Thomas, and spend at least three hours with her best friend. She told Thomas that she wanted to do something special, just for him, and get her hair done. He bought it. Frankie rarely went to the salon. Her hair was so thick and long that it always took forever to get it done, so she would just opt to wash it, and pull it back into a bun.

She walked into the salon, and immediately began to cry when she saw her best friend. Reese grabbed her, and held her close. There were other stylists working on other women's hair, and there were women sitting under the dryers. They were all looking at the two women. Reese grabbed Frankie's hand, and led her to the back office.

"What they hell did he do to you, Frankie?" Reese asked.

"Nothing girl...I'm just really happy to see you."

"I'm happy to see you too sis, but, I think you lying. Spill it."

"Reese, girl, I just don't know about him anymore. I mean, I miss a phone call and he thinks I'm cheating. I don't call him right back, he thinks I don't want to talk to him ever again, and that I'm cheating. He shows up unexpected at my job while I'm out with clients and he assumes I'm having an affair with them. He even accused me of being bi and sleeping with *you*! I just can't deal with it anymore girl. You know, that night at the comedy show he almost got in a fight with some random guy. He accused him of staring at me, and was ready to fight. That was so embarrassing! "

"Leave his ass girl. Simple as that. Not like ya'll got any kids together." Reese was always straight to the point. Never did she give a round about answer for anything. Frankie could count on her to be the one to tell it like it was.

"I don't want to *leave* him. We're supposed to be getting married..."

"So!" Reese was serious.

"It's not that easy, Reese..." Frankie sat down a chair.

"Well then what the hell you wanna do with him? You sound like you're sick of him, so get rid of him. Let him off easy. He's draining you, and ya'll ain't married, no kids, you are free to go, sweetie."

"I know that there's nothing legally tying us together..."

"Then leave!"

"I can't...I need him. He needs me."

"What they hell are you saying? You don't need him, Frankie. You need *you!*"

"Maybe you're right...I'll talk to him tonight. But you still have to do my hair...if I go back home looking like this it will be hell to pay."

"C'mon...I'll hook it up for you." Frankie followed Reese back to the front of the shop, and read a magazine as Reese began to work on her hair. She washed it, placed large rollers in it, and sat her under the dryer. When she was completely done, Frankie's hair looked beautiful. She had long curly locks and Reese had added a very small hint of color highlights to the front. She twirled Frankie around, and Frankie smiled as she saw the face of a woman that she didn't recognize anymore...not because of the hair, but because Thomas was slowly turning her into someone she didn't want to be.

Frankie hugged Reese and promised to hook up with her again real soon. Reese knew that it would be a long time before she saw her best friend again. Frankie left the shop and headed home. Thomas was waiting, of course, when she walked in. He took one look at her hair, and immediately thought that she was doing it for someone else.

"Thomas…how could you say that I got my hair done for someone else? I told you that I did this for you…"

"I don't know about this Frankie…as long as we have been together, you have *never* gotten your hair done like that." Frankie used this opportunity to break it to him that she was done.

"Thomas, look, you are requiring things from me that are impossible for me to deliver on." He looked at her with a blank expression on his face. She continued. "When I met you almost two years ago, I told you that I was not ready for a relationship because I knew how consuming my career was." He never changed his expression. She continued. "My career is my life, and I can't change that. It's my baby, and you know that I love what I do." Frankie sat back and waited for a response. He began to nod his head as if he understood.

"So you telling me you don't want to be with me anymore? Is that what you're saying?"

"Well…" Frankie shrugged her shoulders and looked away.

"Don't try to spare *my* feelings now by trying to sugar coat it. I've been waiting on you to say this for six months now! Is that what you're trying to say?"

"Yes, Thomas! That's what I'm trying to say. I don't want to be with you anymore."

"No." Thomas said blandly.

"No, what?" Frankie was confused.

"No. We are not breaking up and that's that." Thomas explained. Frankie laughed. Thomas had the most serious look on his face to where she actually became nervous.

"How are you going to tell me—"

"Do you love me Frankie?" He cut in.

"Yes, but—"

"There are no buts, Frankie! Either you do or you don't."

"I do. I love you, Thomas. I just don't seem to be able to make you happy."

"Don't tell me if I'm happy or not. Are you in love with me?"

"Yes, I am Thomas, but—"

"Then Frankie please, please don't do this to me. Don't do this to us!" Thomas got on his knees and grabbed her hands. She wasn't expecting him to react like that. She really didn't know how to respond. This was *exactly* why she didn't want to be in a relationship in the first place. It was too much pressure. Too much drama. People get their feelings hurt and she just figured that she would be better off skipping all that.

Needless to say, she reconsidered her choice to break it off with him. With him on his knees and in tears, it was just too much for her to handle. She couldn't go through with it. They talked about why she felt the way she did. She explained to him that he was constantly accusing her of cheating when the idea had *never* even crossed her mind. He expressed why he felt the way he did by explaining to her what Tonya had done to him. Thomas also shared with Frankie that he had been abandoned as a child, and raised by his grandmother who constantly reminded him that he was *not* wanted by anyone and that the *only* reason she kept him was because she would have to answer to the good Lord above if she didn't. Thomas continued to love his grandmother in hopes that one day she would love him back. She never did. Then he looked for love in Tonya, and he felt that he had actually found someone who was going to love him. Then he was overjoyed to find out that he was going to get the opportunity to love a son, and show his son the love that he had never received as a child. His world was turned upside down and destroyed when Tonya and his brother had betrayed him. Learning these things about Thomas allowed Frankie to understand him just a little better. It all made sense as to why he was so skeptical about her cheating, and why he demanded so much of her attention. He had constantly opened his heart throughout his life, and to no avail constantly received it back in ruins.

For the next few weeks, Thomas' attitude improved. Until it was almost as good as it was when they first started dating. Flowers began to arrive at the office more often, and Frankie had made a more conscientious effort to spend more time with him. They began to go on more dates, and Frankie decided to talk with Mike about hiring an additional staff person to help with the work load. Because of how great Frankie's performance was at the company, Mike was able to offer her and the staff additional assistance.

Thomas did have a few setbacks along the way, but for the most part, Frankie felt like he *was* trying. She knew that he was a great guy, it was just that he had some background issues that he needed help dealing with. Frankie wanted to be what he needed. She wanted to support him, and not leave his side like all the others in the past had. She decided that she was going to stand by his side regardless of what trouble lay ahead. She was determined to be devoted to him. She had no idea what she was committing to.

Thirty-Two

FRANKIE WAS RUNNING around with the broom in one hand, and dust spray in the other. She had her earphones in and was jamming to one of her favorite artists playing in her iPod. She was trying to get the house cleaned in time for company. Frankie and Thomas had decided to have a small get together with all their friends at their new home. They had gone ahead and bought a beautiful new home together before the wedding— which was coming up real soon. It was very large and immaculate. Thomas insisted on hiring a maid, but Frankie enjoyed cleaning. It was a high stress reliever. Thomas, being the "man" of the house still hired a maid. However, this day, Frankie had made an executive decision and Wanda, the maid, was off that day.

"But Ms. Frankie…you have a huge party tonight…I have to get the house ready or Mr. Reid will not be happy." Wanda refused to leave.

"Wanda…please go home. You deserve it. I know how to clean a house. Mr. Reid will be just fine. Trust me." Frankie practically pushed Wanda out the door. Frankie slipped into a pair of jogging pants and

Thomas' Cowboys jersey. She tied her hair back into a ponytail, grabbed her iPod, strapped it to her upper arm, and began cleaning.

Thomas came through the front door with his arms full of bags. Frankie was in the bathroom cleaning the toilets, and singing to her self. Thomas called out to get her to come help him. She didn't answer. He called again while he tried to close the door with his right foot. He lost his balance dropping the six-pack of beer that was in his arms. One can burst open, and sprayed all over the foyer. He cursed angrily, and then called for Frankie again. She didn't answer. The rest of the items he had purchased were just about to hit the ground as well, as he tried to gain control. He hollered at the top of his lungs for Frankie as she continued singing. Furious, Thomas dropped everything in his arms, and headed straight for the sound of Frankie's voice.

He looked in the guest bedroom, and didn't see her. He opened the door to the second guest bedroom, and noticed that she wasn't there either. He checked the office. Nothing. But he could still hear her singing her heart out. He climbed the stairs, and turned the corner. There she was, dancing with the broom in the hallway. She jumped when she saw him.

"Oh, baby…you scared me." She said with a smile. Thomas saw nothing but red. He headed straight for her, and grabbed her with both arms. He shook her violently, and pushed her up against the wall. She grabbed his arms, and slapped them off of her. She then pulled her ear phones out of her ears, and looked at him with fear in her eyes.

"What the hell is wrong with you?" She screamed with tears forming in her eyes. Thomas punched the wall next to her head. She jumped.

"YOU DIDN'T HEAR ME SCREAMING FOR YOU?" He yelled.

"NO! Don't you think I would have answered?" She screamed back. Thomas punched the wall again, and made her jump a second time. He had her blocked in between his arms.

"I was screaming, Frankie! And you didn't hear me?" Thomas brought his face in closer to hers, and continued to scream.

"I didn't hear you, okay?" Frankie bent down and crawled out from up under him. "I had my damn earphones in Thomas!" She shoved her earphones up in the air, ran to the bedroom, and locked herself in. For the next half hour, Thomas sat by the door begging her to unlock it. When she finally did, Thomas noticed that her eyes were red and swollen. It was obvious that she had been crying. She backed away from him as he stood up.

"I didn't mean it, Frankie. I swear." He walked up to her, and placed his arms around her. "It won't happen again...I was just frustrated okay. I mean, I had called and called for you and you didn't come and I dropped the beer and it sprayed all"—Frankie was kissing him. "Frankie, baby I'm sorry. I love you..." She kept kissing him.

"I forgive you, baby." Frankie said as she led him to the bed. Frankie believed that he would never do anything to hurt her. She also figured that she would have been just as aggravated had the tables been turned. They ended up on the bed with their clothes off again.

They were interrupted by the door bell. Laughing, they climbed out of the bed, and put on their bath robes. It had to be either Reese or Vincent. They were the only ones who ever showed up on time. Thomas answered the door, and was surprised to find Julian standing there. They hadn't expected Julian because he had said he wasn't coming. The last thing that they needed was for Julian and Reese to go at it again.

"Aye...what's up man?" Julian said as he shook hands, and hugged his frat brother. He took his Kangol off, and looked around the

193

foyer. "Nice crib," Julian said as he took note of the bags and beer all over the floor.

"Thanks. What's good man?" Thomas asked as he began to gather the bags and beer. He walked into the kitchen to grab a wet cloth to clean up the beer that was beginning to dry. "We didn't expect you. Thought you were out of town." Thomas said as he returned with a wet cloth. He finished wiping up the beer, and began to walk to the kitchen to place the cloth in the sink. Julian followed.

"Nah man…my trip was cancelled. I'll be going up there next week."

"Well, look, let me just tell you now, Reese is going to be here tonight dawg and…"

"I gotcha man. I won't even speak to the broad." Thomas shook his head, and snickered. "I'll be right back. Let me get dressed." Thomas ran back upstairs to the bedroom, and found Frankie putting on her clothes. Her body was slightly damp. She had just stepped out of the shower. She looked up at him and grinned. He walked over to her, and kissed her on her back.

"Now, don't start Tommy. We got guests." Frankie warned, and finished getting dressed. While Thomas was in the shower, Frankie went to entertain the first of their guests. She offered Julian a drink and he accepted. He followed her to the kitchen, and took a seat on the bar stool. Julian watched as she made his drink. He could see why Thomas was so into Frankie. She was more than a ten, she was a twenty. Julian continued to observe the shape of her hips, and how the muscles in her calves flexed as she reached up in the cabinet above her head to grab a glass. His eyes roamed all over her body. Thomas' hand on Julian's shoulder broke his focus. He jumped, and tried to play it off.

194

"She fine, ain't she dawg?" Thomas whispered in his ear. He tightened his grip on Julian's shoulder as he eased his hand up closer to his neck. "Don't even imagine what it's like. You touch her, and I'll kill you." Thomas smiled, and walked over to Frankie who was still searching through the cabinets. He placed his hands on her waist while looking back at Julian. Julian had a look of embarrassment covering his face like a mask. Frankie turned to face Thomas. He planted a huge kiss on her lips, and asked if there was something he could help her with—eyeing Julian the whole time.

More guests began to arrive. Music was playing loudly. People were laughing, drinking, and really enjoying themselves. Thomas was at the dinner table playing spades, and Frankie was walking around hosting the party. She stopped and conversed with small groups that were scattered throughout the house. Julian was in the corner talking with a few of his and Thomas' frat brothers from when they both attended Howard. Frankie walked over to see how they were doing on their drinks.

"You guys ok? Need anything?" She placed her hand on Julian's forearm. Thomas looked up from his game, and his blood began to boil.

"Nah, beautiful...we good." Julian answered. Frankie laughed loudly, rested her hand on his chest playfully, and continued to walk on to the next group. Julian watched her as she walked away. He didn't notice Thomas watching him the whole time. By this time, Thomas was livid.

Towards the end of the evening, Reese had turned up the music. She, along with just about everyone else at the party had been drinking. Reese and Frankie may have been drinking just a little too much. Reese began to dance in the middle of the den like she was in the club. Everyone was watching her and some even joined in. She looked around for her sidekick.

"Frankie! Baby where you at, girl?" She yelled over the music. Frankie came stumbling in. Reese grabbed her hand and began to dance with her—moving her arms for her. Reese and Frankie danced, and sang along with the track as they laughed harder than they had ever laughed. Then for some reason, Frankie felt the need to really put on a show—it must have been the alcohol. She cleared off the coffee table, kicked off her shoes, climbed up on it, and began to dance like she was in a strip club. All her guests were laughing and egging her on. She moved her body to the rhythm, and closed her eyes as she touched her body. Reese started pulling out dollar bills, and throwing them at her. The crowd laughed even harder, and joined Reese. Julian felt his man hood rise. He reached into his back pocket and pulled out some money. Frankie was enjoying the attention. Julian walked up to the table as he held out a twenty dollar bill. Frankie played along and danced in front of Julian. Then she leaned down, and with her mouth, grabbed the money from his hand. At that same time, Thomas had gotten up from his card game to see what the fuss was all about. When he saw *his* woman entertaining *his* friend, he became furious, but kept his cool. He stood there in the middle of the entrance, and continued to watch Frankie. Frankie spotted Thomas, and climbed off the table. She walked over to him as seductively as she could without falling over. She placed her hands around his neck as he grabbed her by the wrist tightly while whispering in her ear, "I think you've had enough. It's time for everyone to go now."

Frankie looked into his eyes and could tell that he was not happy. She then turned and signaled for Reese to join her. Reese walked over, and Frankie asked her to turn the music down. Reese pouted and stumbled over to the stereo.

"I would like to thank you all for coming…we have really enjoyed ourselves and hope that you all have as well. It's getting late, and we're going to go ahead and call it a night," Thomas said as he wrapped his arms around the intoxicated Frankie. He shot Julian a sharp stare, and watched as everyone began to gather their things. Thomas pulled Frankie into the foyer by the front door so that they could both say goodnight to their guests. They hugged and kissed their guests as they walked past, one by one. When Julian walked up, Thomas wrapped his hand around the back of Julian's neck and pulled him in close. He whispered in his ear, "Nigga, I told you. How dare you disrespect me like that in *my* house? Don't bring yo' monkey ass round here again or will be looking at the barrel of my gun." Julian pulled back, and gave Thomas an arrogant grin. He leaned over and kissed Frankie on the cheek.

"You two have a good night." Julian said as he placed his Kangol on his head.

"Thanks for coming, Juju. We really enjoyed your company." Frankie said as she waved goodbye. Thomas had already called a cab for Reese and helped her to the car. He gave the driver directions, and paid him.

When the last car and the cab drove off, Frankie closed the door and sighed. "Whew! What a night!" Just then, she felt a sharp blow, and she hit the floor. Thomas had punched her. She placed her hand up to her face, and looked at him shockingly with tears in her eyes.

"How dare you!" He screamed.

"What, Thomas? What?" She cried, still holding her face.

"I can't believe you would disrespect me like that in *our* home!" He grabbed her, jerking her up from the ground. He pulled her into the bedroom.

"What the hell is wrong with you, Tommy! Let me go!" She screamed. He threw her on the bed with such force that her small framed body bounced off the bed. She flipped over the side, and hit her head on the nightstand. She lay on the floor moaning in agony. Thomas, fearful that he may have really hurt her, ran to her side and grabbed her in his arms. He began to rock her and tell her how sorry he was. He was so passive aggressive. Frankie didn't know whether he was coming or going. Happy or angry.

"Frankie, baby I am so sorry. I felt like you and Juju were being too friendly, and then when I saw him sizing you up in the kitchen, and then you put your hand on his chest, and then you were dancing for him, I just couldn't take it anymore!" Thomas pleaded, and explained his case as if he were a child. He knew he was wrong. He began to cry, and his tears began to wet Frankie's face.

Frankie reached her arms up around his neck with the small amount of strength she had. She lay in his arms, head pounding, and cried with him. She knew that this was just another block in the road to his healing from what Tonya and his grandmother had done to him. Frankie knew that it would be hard…but not this hard. *He's only acting like this because he thinks you are going to do him like Tonya did him. If you just love him and stay devoted…he will come around.* He was having a hard time letting the past be the past, and he was obviously making her pay for Tonya's mistakes. Frankie loved Thomas, and felt that she was going to stand by him, and help him through this. She felt that if she could prove to him that she wasn't out to hurt him and that she desperately loved him then he wouldn't be so skeptical. Then, he would trust her.

Frankie woke up the next morning with a huge headache. She probably had a concussion but didn't feel like it was bad enough to have to go to the hospital, so she decided to stay in bed. She noticed that Thomas wasn't in bed. *He must have gone to the gym.* Then she smelt bacon cooking. Within minutes, Thomas appeared with a tray of breakfast, and placed it on the bed. He wanted to make it up to her for what happened the night before. She sat up and allowed him to serve her. She smiled knowing that with a little reassurance, and maybe even counseling, Thomas would be fine. Maybe she *was* being a little over the top last night, and maybe she *was* being a little too friendly with Julian. Her intentions were never to hurt Thomas, and she wanted to make sure that he knew this.

She ate her breakfast while Thomas stepped out of the room. Not too soon after that, he showed up with flowers in his hand. He had her favorite—tulips. She gasped at the sight of them, and thanked him. From that day on, Thomas' actions became more unpredictable, and before Frankie knew it, she was walking on eggshells—again.

Thirty-Three

FRANKIE HAD CLIMBED to one of the highest levels in her company. She was landing large accounts left and right. Mr. Wallace was genuinely impressed with her performance, and had promoted her to Senior Manager of Executive Accounts. At this level, she would be simply guiding her team to procure and retain accounts like she had done so effortlessly. She had a large client presentation, and brought Gary and Patrice with her to observe her tactics.

"Ms. Leone, I believe that your expertise and your innovative ideas are just what we are looking for." Mr. Montgomery of Yoko International, Inc. said as he rose from his chair.

"I am very please to hear that, sir. I love what I do, and I feel that the only way to do it right is to allow my passion to be visible in every aspect of my work." Frankie stood up as well, and began to place her portfolio in its case.

"We will be in touch, Ms. Leone. I do expect to have our Southern Region branch up and running within the next few months, and I would love to have your company take over our retirement accounts, and possibly handle our mutual funds."

"It would be my pleasure, Mr. Montgomery. I am confident that you will not be disappointed." Frankie shook Mr. Montgomery's outstretched hand, and smiled. She wanted to scream at the top of her lungs, but she maintained her cool. Gary and Patrice watched closely with admiration in their eyes. They loved Frankie. There wasn't the slightest bit of jealously for her. She bent down to grab her briefcase, and felt light-headed. She tried to shake it off, and walk slowly to her car. She waved goodbye to Mr. Montgomery…and that was the last thing she remembered doing.

"Frankie…Frankie…" Frankie could barely open her eyes. Her head was pounding. She managed to open them, and saw Thomas standing over her. She looked around but couldn't focus.

"What…what…what happened?" She asked.

"You passed out in the parking lot of Yoko International. Gary and Patrice called me." Thomas began to rub her forehead. Frankie immediately began to back-track. She couldn't remember if she had completed the presentation with Mr. Montgomery or if she had passed out afterwards. Thomas reassured her that everything was fine, and reminded her that she had actually won the deal. She was a little relieved, but then became concerned at whether or not she had embarrassed herself by passing out in from of a mega high-end client. Her head hurt too badly to worry too much about it, so she let it go.

The doctor walked in with his tablet and a file in his hands. He closed the door behind him. "Oh, Ms. Leone, I see that you have awakened from your nap. How was la-la land?" He took a quick glance at Frankie's pupils, and then began to read his clip board. "I've got some great news…you are going to live." He chuckled a dry laugh to himself and looked at Thomas and Frankie in hopes that they would join him. Frankie just smiled, and Thomas kept his eyes on Frankie. The doctor continued. "And the baby is doing fine."

"*BABY?*" Both Thomas and Frankie screamed together. The doctor looked confused at their reaction.

"Yes. Baby. Ms. Leone, you are close to two months pregnant. More ultrasounds and tests will give a more accurate measurement." The doctor sat down at his desk, and began to type. Thomas and Frankie sat in amazement and shock. *A baby? Are we ready?*

Thomas reached over and grabbed her hand. He was so excited and wanted to scream. Frankie was unsure how to feel. She forced an excited expression to show on her face. The beatings had gotten worse, and she was fearful for her life at that point. They had good and bad days. The good days were really great, and the bad days were horrible. Frankie couldn't make eye contact with someone of a different sex. She had even begun to cut Reese off because there were times when Thomas had accused Frankie of sleeping with her. Thomas had become more insecure to the point that he didn't even like when June would call.

"I don't care if he's your cousin. He calls too damn much. Something is not right about it!" He would say. And every time June would call, he would lie and say she was in the shower, or sleep.

Thomas began to require more and more of her time—more than before. He called constantly while she was at work, and expected her to stay on the phone with him for hours at a time. Frankie would have to beg to get off because, God forbid she hang up the phone. She would surely feel the effects of her actions once she got home.

Then she thought that maybe this child would cause him to calm down. But then on the other side of it, this child would connect her to

Thomas for life and she, at the point, was ready to call it quits. She thought about the night that she could have walked away but chose to go back. She and Thomas had just gotten in from the movie theater. Out of the blue, Thomas began to accuse her of cheating on him with Vincent.

"Vincent? C'mon Thomas, now you're being crazy!" Frankie screamed as she placed her purse down. She tried to be careful with her tone because the slightest change would make him flip out.

"Crazy? Crazy?" Thomas began screaming. "You're calling me crazy?" He began to walk towards her. Frankie began to back away, and tried to run. He chased her, attacking her from behind. He tackled her to the ground. He flipped her over, and began to punch her in her face. She tried her best to block the blows, and wiggle out of his grip. He then ripped her clothes off, pull himself out of his pants, and forced himself inside of her. She begged him to stop. He did, surprisingly. With a blank stare, he moved to the side and let her up. She stood up quickly and slid her pants back on. She was crying profusely, and was having trouble composing herself. She walked to the kitchen to grab a paper towel to wipe the blood off her face. Thomas came up behind her, and grabbed her crotch. "I know why you want me to stop. You don't want me to know that you don't curve to me anymore! You *have* been sleeping with Vinny!"

Frankie grabbed the kitchen knife that was on the counter and turned to face him. His expression did not change. He did back away though. She dropped the knife, and headed for the door. Luckily, he had forgotten to close it all the way. She ran as fast as she could into the street. She ran down the rode in her bare feet, and spotted a patrol car coming around the corner. She had stopped him, and asked for them to help her. They allowed her to crawl into the back seat of the car, and took her to the station. They ended up calling Anthony for her. As she waited in an interrogation room for Anthony to show up, she continued to cry. She thought about how she could get to her parent's house. She knew that she couldn't go back to her house because Thomas would probably kill her. Anthony stepped into the cold room.

"Key-Lime! Damn girl…your face! What happened to your face?" Anthony asked as he touched her face. She flinched. "How long has he been beating you, Key?" Frankie didn't respond. "Frankie, how long?" Anthony pleaded. Tears filled his eyes but he remained calm.

"I lost count…I don't know anymore." Tears began to roll down her bloody face.

"We can go arrest him, Frankie. You just gotta say the word," Anthony said. Frankie declined, and wouldn't give Anthony any reason as to why she didn't want to press charges. She felt in her heart that he was truly going through some things, and she felt guilty for even thinking about pressing charges or leaving him. Thomas didn't have any close family that he could depend on, and even those he had called friends were becoming more and more distant. *Who else is going to stand by his side?* It was apparent. Frankie had fallen in to the cycle of an abusive lifestyle. She was afraid to leave Thomas. She knew that it would just destroy him. Not only that, but it could possibly risk her life. She was afraid to stay in fear that she may crack one of the eggshells that she frequently walked upon. She looked at Anthony, and felt more pain. Here this man was, indisputably concerned about her, and she was worried about abandoning Thomas. Anthony loved Frankie, really loved Frankie, and she couldn't see it. It hurt Anthony to see her like that. He drove her to her parent's house, and kissed her on the cheek. She stepped out, still barefoot and walked into the house. Thomas was standing there waiting for her. Begging her to forgive him and asking her to come home. Frankie climbed into his car and, rode home with him. Now, sitting in the doctor's office, Frankie wished that she would have never gone back.

Frankie's belly began to grow along with Thomas' insecurity. He counted down the days that led to the day she would deliver this child. He stood on the sidelines, skeptical, and anticipating the news that this woman too, had done the same thing as Tonya.

Frankie began to get used to the little life that kept moving inside her. Ever so often, she would place her hands on her stomach, and say a small prayer. She was torn between the love that was growing for her unborn child, and the hate that was also forming inside of her thanks to the angry hands of Thomas. She was afraid for her child's life as well. She didn't want to bring this child into such a dysfunctional lifestyle. *This baby didn't ask to be here.* And Frankie felt horrible knowing that she was not stopping it. She thought about terminating the pregnancy, but couldn't bring herself to do it. The day that Reese took her to the clinic, she almost threw up when the nurse went over the procedure.

"Now Ms. Leone, we need you to put this gown on, and take off everything else. I will return in a few minutes." The nurse said as she and Reese left the room. Reese looked back at her dear friend. Both of them with tears in their eyes.

Frankie took off all her clothes, and rubbed her stomach. She walked over to the mirror that was hanging on the wall by the door, and stood there looking at her naked, and bruised body. The large bruise on her chest reminded her of why she was doing this. The handprints on her ankles from when Thomas dragged her through the house in one of his fits, reminded her of how innocent *this* child was. The bruises on her ribs made her think of the freedom she once had before she allowed Thomas to cloud her vision, and her judgment. She stood there, in tears, and began to put the paper gown on. She walked back over to the table, and climbed up on it. The nurse walked in, asked her to lie down, scoot her bottom to the end of the table, and place her feet in the stirrups. The nurse noticed the bruises on Frankie's ankles, and thought to herself that Frankie was doing the right thing. A doctor walked in, spoke briefly to them both, and Frankie then heard him turn on a machine which sounded like a vacuum cleaner. Her stomach fluttered, and when the doctor touched her knee, she immediately sat up. Tears streaming down her face, she cried, "I can't do this!" She stood up, and jumped off the table. She grabbed her clothes, shoes, and ran to the nearest bathroom.

Reese saw her leave the room, and ran to follow her as she disappeared into the bathroom. She heard Frankie hysterically crying in the far back stall. Reese walked over and placed her hand on the door.

"Frankie, baby. I'm here." Reese's eyes filled with tears as her friend cried her heart out. Minutes later the stall door opened and Frankie stood there in all her clothes. She shrugged her shoulders, and with a sad grin, she spread her arms as if she were showing off her outfit and said, "I couldn't do it. I just couldn't do it Reese."

Frankie decided that she was going to accept this child, and prepare for the arrival. She still had the chance to terminate, but still was not able to bring herself to do it. She decided that she would go downtown to buy a few things, hoping that it would ease her mind. She met Yahira for brunch, and then left her behind to do some shopping and soul searching alone. Thomas was at his office, so she took advantage of the opportunity to get away from him. She spent about three hours browsing different boutiques, but just wasn't feeling up to shopping. She felt good to just be alone, out of the office, and the house. She figured she would just take a walk throughout the town and enjoy the great weather.

Desperately Devoted

As she walked past a little café, her stomach rumbled, and she decided to make a quick pit stop to grab a small bite to eat. She walked into the café, and saw a small table next to a window. She grabbed the seat, and waited for the waitress to come and take her order. As she continued to review the menu, she felt someone standing next to her. Without looking up, assuming it was the waitress, she began to place her order.

"I look like I work here?" The man's voice startled her. She looked up to see Julian standing there with a huge grin on his face.

"Juju! Hey you! How have you been? Please, have a seat!" She pointed to the empty chair across from her. Julian's presence brought an easy feeling over her. He kissed her on the cheek, and sat down. "What's been going on with you? Man, Juju, I haven't seen you since our party last year."

"I'm *good*. The question is: how are *you* doing?" Julian looked concerned. Frankie became uncomfortable. She hated when others tried to talk to her about Thomas. When she explained her reasons for staying with him, everyone would always look at her like she was a fool. She was beginning to *feel* like she was a fool too.

"I'm fine." She answered sharply.

"Don't lie, Frankie. I know how he is. You need to be careful." Julian placed his hand on hers, and looked into her eyes.

"Julian, don't worry about me. I am a big girl, and know how to take care of myself."

"Apparently not." He pointed to his own collar bone. Frankie looked down, and saw that one of her latest bruises was peeking out from the edge of her blouse. *I thought I covered it up with make-up!* She readjusted her shirt, and shifted in her seat uncomfortably.

The waitress approached the table, and proceeded to take Frankie's order. When she looked at Julian, he pushed back from the table, and stood up. Placing the chair back under the table he leaned over and kissed Frankie on the forehead.

"I was just leaving, ma'am. I won't be having anything." The waitress flipped her pad shut and walked off. "Frankie, there are people out here that *do* care about you, and are worried about you. Please be careful." Julian placed his hand on her shoulder. Pain shot through her whole body. That was a fresh spot, too. She jumped slightly. Julian shook his head.

Placing her hand on his that was still rested on her shoulder, she looked up at him and smiled. "I'll be fine, Juju. Thanks for checking on me." Julian left the café. He looked both ways before crossing the street, placed his Kangol on his head, and ran across to get in his car. Off to the right, was Thomas, parked in his Mercedes, piping hot. He had watched the whole interaction from the driver's seat of his car in disbelief—tears streaming, and rage building. He drove home, and waited for his fiancé to walk through the door.

Frankie slid her keys into the lock, and the door flew open. Thomas was standing there in his boxers. He had a look in his eye that scared the hell out of Frankie. She didn't know what she could have possibly done. She was shopping all day. Wanda had cleaned the house. It wasn't time for dinner. She racked her brain within a matter seconds trying to figure out what today's beating would be for.

Thomas grabbed her and pulled her into the house. He stuck his head out the front door, and looked around trying to spot any nosy neighbors. He closed the door and turned to face a terrified Frankie.

"Thomas. You're scaring me. What's wrong?" She pleaded. Thomas reached his arm back and slapped Frankie. He was so strong and the force from this one caused her body to turn completely around. She slid across the foyer, on her stomach. The pressure from the blow to her belly caused her to throw up. Thomas stood over her, and began to kick her mercilessly. She begged for him to stop. She tried to get up on all fours but he kicked her again.

"I CAN'T BELIEVE YOU! HOW COULD YOU, FRANKIE! HOW COULD YOU!" Thomas yelled as he continued to kick her. She crawled down the hallway crying the entire time.

"Thomas! What are you talking about?"

"YOU KNOW WHAT I'M TALKING ABOUT! I KNEW IT ALL ALONG! YOU AND JULIAN! THAT'S HIS DAMN BABY AIN'T IT? AIN'T IT?" Thomas kicked her again.

"Juju? Baby, no!" She figure at that moment that he must have been following her and saw them at the café.

"I SAW YOU! I SAW YOU WITH HIM TODAY!" Thomas began to cry. Pain struck his heart. Guilt, once again, struck hers. She understood what was going on now. She did her best to console him. Crying uncontrollably now, Thomas threw himself up against the wall, and slid down. He began to sob in his hands. Frankie struggled to pull herself up from the ground, and she crawled over to her man. She grabbed his head and held him. He grabbed her, and cried in her breasts. She continued to hold him as blood began to form between her legs, underneath her.

Thirty-Four

FRANKIE SAT ON the hospital bed with tears streaming down her face. She had just lost her baby, but she was relieved that she didn't have to raise that innocent child in a home full of violence and fear. She was so unsure of how to really feel. The curtains opened, and in stepped Anthony, dressed in full uniform.

"Tony…" Frankie was happy to see him.

"Frankie, I *know* you are going to do it this time. You've got to." Anthony pleaded. He hated to see her living like this. He knew that this was not who she really was.

"Tony…you don't understand." Frankie looked down at her bare feet.

"You're right, I don't understand Frankie! I don't understand *why* you would allow this man to treat you like this. You don't realize that every time you come to this hospital, and they suspect abuse, they call us. I have heard *every* incident over the radio. I don't understand how you can live like this. *That's* what I don't understand." Anthony grabbed her hands, and tried to get her to look into his eyes.

"He needs me!" She cried.

"YOU need you, Frankie! What happened to you? What happened to the strong black woman I knew?" Anthony looked so hurt, and disappointed. He stood closer to her side and wiped the tears from her face.

"I don't know Tony. I don't know what happened to her..."

Thirty-Five

FRANKIE PULLED UP in the driveway and noticed that Thomas' car wasn't there. She sighed. It was a relief to not have to come home to deal with him right now. She didn't know how he was going to handle hearing that she had lost the baby. That conversation could go many ways. He would either accept it and then try for another one, or he would break down and have a pity party blaming himself for killing the baby—which Frankie *did* believe was his fault. Or he would flip out and accuse her of losing it on purpose. Either way, she wasn't in the mood to deal with it. She wished that she had the courage to really leave him, but the guilt trips that he would play on her were hard for her to handle. And Thomas knew it.

She climbed into the tub and soaked for practically an hour. When she got out, she poured herself and glass of wine and chased it with the pain medication that the doctor prescribed for her. It wasn't long afterwards, she felt herself getting sleepy. She wobbled back to the bedroom and threw herself on the bed. The room got blurry and she passed out.

Frankie woke to Thomas violently shaking her and screaming. *Please not tonight!* She opened her eyes to see his face about one inch from hers. She couldn't understand what he was saying.

"Huh?" she mumbled.

"Why are you drinking? Are you *trying* to kill our baby?" He had the empty wine glass in his hands. Frankie rubbed her eyes.

"Thomas they baby is already dead! I lost the baby today! Remember? You kept kicking me in my stomach!" She screamed. Thomas backed away from her slowly. *Oh no...I didn't mean for it to come out like that.* His facial expression changed. His eyes filled with pain and heartache. He dropped the wine glass and fell to the ground sobbing. Frankie felt horrible. She didn't want to break it to him that way, but it slipped out. She pulled herself up and walked over to him. She assumed her normal position, and rocked the crying grown man in her arms all night.

Thirty-Six

FRANKIE PULLED UP into her parents' driveway, excited to see them, and excited be home. Thomas was on a month long trip to Paris on business and Frankie was elated that he was gone. The wedding was still supposed to happen in the next couple of weeks and Frankie was allowing her mother to coordinate all the details. Frankie didn't care anymore if they got married in Montego Bay or in Timbuktu. She just didn't care anymore, period.

Thomas was nervous about leaving her behind while he traveled, but knew that it was impossible to get her to come with him. She had a great position at Wallace NVest, but not great enough to where she could go away for over a month. So he sucked it up, and hoped that he could trust her. To try and ease his worries, she gave him *the best* loving she had ever given him before. She wanted to make sure that he didn't try to rearrange his plans in order to stay behind.

She walked through the front door and through the house briskly, in search for her mother. She found her on the back porch on the swing.

214

As soon as she laid her eyes on her mother she broke down in tears. Her mother sat up and gawked at her daughter. Frankie walked over to her mother who was still seated on the cushioned patio swing. Frankie sat down nest to her mother.

"Frankie, darling, what's wrong?" She asked Frankie.

"Mother…I don't know what to do with my life anymore. I have completely let it get out of control." Frankie kept crying.

"What do you mean, honey?"

"Thomas…he…he beats me." She looked up at her mother, expecting her to console her and make it all go away.

"Frankie…what are you doing to make him want to beat you? You are weeks away from this wedding. Sweetie, we don't have time for drama." Her mother's words stunned her. Frankie couldn't understand why she would say something like that. But then again, she had to consider the source. Vivian had one thing on her mind—money.

"What? Where's Daddy?" Frankie stood up.

"Your father is in California. Come with me, I want you to see the bouquets that I've selected for you. They are all to die for, and I can't decide, so you need to." Vivian stood up, and reached her hand out towards Frankie. Frankie stood there, stunned. "Look, we are not going to deal with you and your temper tantrums sweetheart. Thomas is a good man. I've met him, and I can tell that he is going to take very good care of you. The *only* reason he could have possibly put in hands on you would have to be because you *did* something. Now…whatever it is that you're doing…stop it. You have been desperately searching for a man that will provide for you and now that you have a good one, you want to have a little tantrum. Grow up Frankie! Now, come. Bouquets." Vivian pulled Frankie's arm. Frankie snatched away, still stunned. Frankie backed away from her mother. Her mother's words hurt worse than any blow from

Thomas. With tears in her eyes, she walked towards the front door. Her mother tried to stop her to figure out what it was that she had said to upset Frankie. "Frankie, darling, we have a deadline to make!" Vivian really didn't "get it". Frankie said good bye, and drove off, leaving her unsympathetic, confused mother standing in the driveway.

"Fine. I'll pick the bouquet out myself!" Vivian huffed and stormed back into the house. Frankie drove down the long highway, daydreaming about disappearing, and never looking back. Thomas wouldn't be back for another month and by the time he got back, she could be long gone. Her cell phone rang, interrupting her thoughts.

"Hello." She said between sniffs.

"Hey Key-Lime." It was Anthony. "I just wanted to check on you." His voice brought her a sense of peace.

"I'm good T-Bird." She sniffed.

"Well you don't sound like it. Word on the street is that Thomas is in Paris. Is that true?"

"Wow, word sure travels fast huh?" She wiped her eyes.

"You musta forgot, I'm a cop. I can find out anything." He laughed. "Well at least you will get a break."

"Yeah." She agreed. Anthony was surprised that she didn't begin lecturing him, going on and on about how he didn't understand, and how Thomas needed her, and so on.

"Well, I just wanted to check on you. Not gonna hold you." Frankie didn't want him to hang up. "Call me if you need anything. And Key-Lime, I mean *anything*."

Frankie wanted so badly to be in Anthony's arms. She thought back to how happy he used to make her. She thought of how tender his words were. She thought of how genuine he was. She picked up the phone and called him back.

"Tony...I really need to talk." Frankie's voice began to quiver. Anthony knew, from the sound of her voice, that she really needed someone...at that moment.

"Where are you?"

"Driving back from McLean...going home." Frankie wiped away a tear.

"I'll be home in a few minutes. Can you meet me at my place?"

"Yes...I'll be there in twenty."

"Okay...see you in a bit." Anthony hung up the phone, and drove home to meet her. Frankie was relieved.

Anthony was waiting patiently on the front steps of his townhouse as Frankie drove up. He stood up, and watched her climb out of her car. She walked solemnly up to him. He greeted her immediately with a hug. Tears flooded Frankie's eyes as she allowed Anthony to comfort her. He pulled away, grabber her hand, and led her into his home. He led her to his living room, and they both sat down on his plush, hunter green sectional couch. Frankie looked around the tidy space, and was impressed at how exquisite his taste was. Frankie closed her eyes, and lay back on the huge pillows. With tears in her eyes, she began to apologize.

"Tony...I have to tell you that I am so sorry. I am so sorry for being shallow, and breaking your heart. I thought that having a man that could buy me this, and buy me that, just like my daddy did, was what I needed." Tears began to fall from her eyes. Anthony reached behind him and pulled a tissue from a tissue box that was resting on the coffee table. He began to wipe the tears from her face as she continued. "I was looking at monetary things. Things that meant absolutely nothing! And I felt that you would never be able to provide those things for me...I was wrong to do you the way I did." Anthony reached up and placed his hand behind her head. He moved in closer as compassion began to fill his eyes. "Tony, I am asking you to please forgive me. I am so sorry and I just want you to know that."

Anthony smiled. For years, those were the only words that he had ever wanted to hear her to say. He had forgiven her years ago and had never stopped praying for her. He still loved her as much now as he did then.

"Frankie, I forgave you years ago. It really feels good to hear those words from you. It really means a lot to me. Thank you."

Thirty-Seven

FRANKIE AND ANTHONY had such a wonderful evening the night they went to dinner. After dinner, they took a long walk in the park, reminiscing about life back in high school. They ended up holding hands, and didn't realize that they were doing it. They both looked at each other, and laughed. They walked further, and stopped at a pond—the same pond that Greg had poured his heart out when he had presented Frankie with that fake promise ring.

The moon was shinning off the water creating an ambiance so peaceful and serene. They took a seat on the grass, and leaned their shoulders up against each other—like they used to do when they were dating in high school. Anthony looked into her eyes, and practically begged her to leave Thomas.

"Frankie, you don't have to stay there. You know that. You deserve so much better. It's not like you *need* money. And all those other things that money *can't* buy, you aren't getting that anyways. And those things aren't hard to get, nor are they too much to ask for. I can love you, Frankie. I *still* love you, Frankie. I have never stopped loving you.

Frankie, please let me love you." Anthony pleaded. By now, he was completely turned, facing her. Frankie's eyes softened as she tilted her head sideways.

"Tony, I can't—"

"Shhhhhh…don't say anything. Just know this…know that I love you. You apparently aren't ready for love." He paused, and Frankie thought about what he had just said. Up until this point, she had always believed that Thomas *did* love her, but his kind of love hurt. His kind of love made her uncomfortable, and uneasy. Anthony stood up, still looking into her eyes and said, "Frankie, when you are ready to love yourself, *then* you will be ready for love. And when you are ready for love, you know how to find me." Tony kissed her on the forehead, and walked off. Frankie spent the next few hours, in tears, alone, with only her thoughts, by the pond.

Thirty-Eight

THE WEEK THAT THOMAS was supposed to come home, Frankie became tense. She dreaded the fact that her peace was going to come to an end within a matter of days. It really saddened her. She had been spending more time with Anthony, and hated the fact that those days were soon coming to an end as well. The past couple of weeks were the happiest that she had experienced in a long time. She could be herself around Anthony. She could laugh as loudly as she wanted. She could even watch movies with Anthony, and not worry that she would end up in a fist fight for her life because he felt like she was fantasizing about the sexy actors on the screen. The nights that she spent with Tony were surely ones that she would cherish forever.

Lying in his arms, listening to the rain coming down outside as he recited poems to her, made her wish that she could lay there forever. She somehow wished that Thomas' flight would get delayed for say, five years, or forever. *Maybe he can get lost at sea...*

Frankie listened to Anthony:

The day our souls collided, and connected

Our physical beings continued on with life

But our souls began to form solid ties

Ties that would bind us with the strength of love

The love that would absorb all pain

The pain that we suffered at the hands of others

Others who were *never* worthy

Worthy of our minds, our bodies, our souls

Because when our souls

Collided

We became one.

Anthony looked over at Frankie. Frankie had tears in her eyes. He wiped them away.

"That was beautiful, Tony. Thank you for sharing that with me."

"I wrote that the day I met you." Anthony placed the paper down on the floor, and rubbed his hands through Frankie's hair. He pulled her face in closer to his.

"Tony, that's so beautiful." Frankie's eyes softened.

"You're beautiful." Anthony kissed her on the nose. They both lay there in each others arms as they had done the night they both experience sex together for the first time…as teenagers. Anthony lightly ran his hands across her arms, her hips, her thighs, and legs. He held her hands, and kissed her again. He looked at her as if it was his first time he had ever seen her. She allowed him to do with her body whatever he desired. For that moment, she really felt loved. She knew that if no one loved her, Anthony did. She just knew that there wouldn't be anyway that they could really work because of how badly she had hurt him years ago.

That night, Anthony focused on pleasing Frankie, and showing her how much she *still* meant to him.

Thirty-Nine

IT WAS CLOSE TO five o'clock, and Frankie had a few emails that she needed to respond to. She also had a client that she was supposed to meet for dinner in thirty minutes. She finished what she was in the middle of, and headed out the door. Half way down the road her cell phone rang.

"Frankie Leone speaking."

"Where the hell are you Frankie?" It was Thomas, and she had forgotten that she was supposed to be meeting *him* this evening for dinner. He had just gotten in from Paris. She had the dates wrong on the calendar, and had double-booked her meeting with a very important client.

"Oh my goodness sweetie, I completely forgot! Baby I am so sorry. I have to meet with a client in fifteen minutes for"—Click. He hung up. *I don't have time for this!* She continued to drive towards the restaurant while trying to get him back on the phone. Frankie continued to press redial but didn't get an answer. Then she texted him: ANSWER YOUR PHONE! He responded: HELL NO! She threw the phone in the passenger side seat, and proceeded to park her car in the lot of Fiestas

Mexican Bar and Grill. She grabbed her laptop, purse, and went inside. She figured that she would breeze right through her presentation, and still have time to meet Thomas. She left the phone right there in the seat…purposely.

Walking inside the restaurant, she spotted a middle aged guy sitting at a table towards the middle of the room. She walked over, and asked, "Are you Daniel Peterson?" He looked up at her.

"Yes?"

"Hello, Mr. Peterson, I'm Frankie Leone. Nice to finally meet in person." She extended her hand. He stood up, and shook it. He was very handsome and clean cut.

"It sure is. All this phone tag stuff was starting to get old. *Really* nice to meet you. Please…have a seat." She set her laptop on the floor, and sat down. They made small talk as they waited for the waitress to come and take their orders. They ordered appetizers, and got straight to business. Halfway through their meeting, Frankie felt someone standing over her, and she noticed Mr. Peterson looking up. Frankie turned around, and there stood Thomas, with the coldest look in his eyes. Fear gripped her heart. The last thing she needed was for Thomas to have one of his "fits" right there in public…in front of a client.

"Thomas, what are you doing here?" Frankie said trying to sound pleasantly surprised as a nervous smile formed on her pale face.

"Frankie, can I see you for a minute?" Thomas' eyes were filled with anger.

"Mr. Peterson, please excuse me." Mr. Peterson nodded his head but kept staring at them. Thomas grabbed Frankie's arm really hard, and they both began to walk towards the exit. "Thomas, you're hurting me!" She said in a low tone without trying to make a scene. She tried to pull away from him, but he clutched tighter. They made it to the exit, and he pushed her outside. She turned to face him.

"What the—"

"I knew it!" he hollered.

"You knew what Thomas?" She looked around to see if anyone was watching.

"I *knew* you were cheating! You are so trifling! I can't believe you! I go away on business…business…so that I can bring more money into the household so that *you* won't have to work anymore…and this is how you repay me?"

"Thomas, what the hell are you talking—"

"Business meeting, huh? Client my ass! I thought you were special, Frankie! I thought you were different! You're just like the rest of them! Whores! You're all whores!"

"Thomas! Stop! I'm serious! He *is* a client! Have I *ever* given you a reason not to trust me?" Thomas was silent. "No, I haven't! And you continue to make me pay for Tonya's mistakes."

"No I'm not! Just because I was in Paris didn't mean that I didn't have eyes here! And don't *ever* bring Tonya up again!"

"What are you talking about?" Frankie was completely confused.

"You were seen having dinner with some guy…and taking a long walk in the park…and holding hands…and watching the moon…I can't get you to do that with *me*!"

"Thomas, he was just a—" She tried to defend herself. She knew that he was talking about her dinner date with Anthony, but nothing happened—not *that* night. It was just dinner and conversation. But there was no way that Thomas was going to believe that.

226

"Just a friend, huh? Fine. Fine, Frankie. You got it. Maybe I'm crazy." Thomas' voice changed. No longer was he screaming. He was speaking calmly at that point.

"Thomas, you have really crossed the line this time. I am in the middle of a business meeting with a highly respected client of mine! I don't have time for—"

"You never have time! You never have time!" Thomas sneered at her, walked off to his car, and drove out of the lot with his tires squealing.

Frankie did her best to compose herself before walking back inside to finish her dinner meeting. She would just have to face the harsh consequences when she got home, but right now, she needed to focus on her client.

Mr. Peterson looked up at her as she approached the table. "Please forgive me. I apologize for that." She said as she sat back down, and took a sip of her water.

"Everything ok?" He looked concerned.

"Oh...yes. Everything is fine. Just a little mix-up. But everything is fine. Now, where were we?"

Dinner lasted for about another twenty minutes. Frankie closed the deal, and sent Mr. Peterson off, a happy man. *Yes! One in the bucket for me! I love my job!*

Frankie took the long route home. When she pulled up she noticed that all the lights were off. She dreaded putting her key in that lock. She turned the door knob, and walked inside. Instantly she felt hands grip around her throat like a python, and the quick jolt caused her to drop her keys. She struggled, and scratched at the hands around her throat. She tried to scream, but the pressure was so tense on her windpipe, that nothing would come out. Then her head hit the wall with such force that she literally saw stars. Then, she felt her body lift from the ground. Her

feet were dangling, and her vision was becoming blurred. She
continuously slapped at Thomas' arms in a desperate cry for mercy. The
love in his eyes had transformed to pure hatred. Frankie placed both hands
on his wrists that were fixed tightly around her throat. "P—please!
Please...I...can't...breathe." She was barely able to get the words out.
Then, he dropped her. She gasped for air as she rubbed her throat.

"You slept with him didn't you!" Thomas yelled. Frankie
couldn't think straight. She was still in shock. She crawled towards the
couch so that she could pull herself up. Then she felt a huge blow to her
head. The hit was so hard that it knocked her onto her back. The pain in
her head was excruciating, and growing. She begged for him to stop.
With every muscle in her body, she tried to turn back over, and crawl
towards the door. Another blow. This time to her ribs. A sharp pain shot
through to her back, and she threw up...dejá vu. Thomas disappeared
momentarily, and Frankie tried to make a run for the door. Just before she
made it to the door, Thomas stood in front of her. With tears streaming
down her face, on her hands and knees, she looked up at him. Her mouth
opened, and terror ripped through her soul instantly. She raised her hand
to beg him to stop. "T-homas...please...don't!" Before she could say
anything else, the gun went off.

Forty

EVERYTHING SOUNDED LIKE she was under water. Frankie tried to make out what the voice was saying.

"Frankie…Frankie…Frankie…" Frankie could hear someone calling her name but she couldn't open her eyes. She tried to answer but something was in her throat that prevented her from speaking. "Frankie? It's me, Reese. C'mon baby, open your eyes. I'm here." Reese pleaded. Frankie struggled to open her eyes. "That's it baby. Come on." She was rooting for her like always. Frankie opened her eyes to see Reese's face. Frankie tried to speak again, but couldn't.

"Yo! Doc!" Reese turned her head towards the door, and screamed. "Get in here, and get this tube out my sister's throat! She's trying to talk!" *Tube? Down my throat? Where the hell am I? Last I thing that I remember…oh my God.* All Frankie could think was *I'm not dead? I'm not dead! Why didn't you let me die God?*

The nurses came running in, and asked Reese to move. One nurse placed her hand on Frankie's chest. The nurse placed a syringe into the tube to deflate the cuff, and then asked Frankie to cough. As Frankie tried coughing, the nurse pulled the tube out of her throat. Frankie rubbed her throat, and closed her eyes again. For the next few minutes, the nurses were checking her eyes, mouth, blood pressure, and every other machine they had her plugged up to. Frankie just lay there, watching the show. When they were done, they left the room so that she could be alone with her guest. Her throat was very sore so she couldn't talk much, but she was very was happy to see Reese's face. Reese's appearance had changed drastically. All her piercings were gone, her hair was one color, and she had it pulled back in a very classy bun. The outfit she had on was similar to that which Frankie would have chosen to wear. There was something different about Reese altogether.

"Reese Pieces..." Frankie whispered.

Reese smiled, and sat on the bed. "Yes?"

"Where is he?" Frankie asked. Reese's face changed.

"Let's not talk about him...okay." Reese patted Frankie's hand. "I need you to get better. We got Jamaica coming up soon, remember?" Frankie and Reese had made plans to take a vacation to Jamaica with all their friends. Thomas had approved it, and Frankie was so excited about going.

"Reese, please..." Frankie grunted, and grabbed her throat.

"Hey, Key-Lime," Anthony said as he walked closer to the bed. Frankie turned her head to the left to look at him. Seeing his face made the pain go away for a brief moment.

"Sup, cuzzo!" June called out from behind Reese. Frankie turned her head back to the right to see her favorite cousin standing there looking at her lovingly. Just then, the room door flew open, and in burst Frankie's father with teddy bear's and flowers. "Hey Reese...how's Frankie—

AAAHHH!!!" He screamed. "My pumpkin pie is awake!!! Vivian! Frankie is awake!" He threw the teddy bears down, and ran over to the bed. Her mother's voice stopped him in his tracks, Frankie sighed in relief, because he was probably going to try to pick her up.

"Shelton! Be careful with her!" Vivian walked in. Her nose was turned up as usual, and she was dressed like she had just stepped out of Vogue. Vivian looked at Reese, and rolled her eyes. She still had a problem with Reese, even after all these years. She then looked at Frankie, and walked elegantly over to the bed. Frankie couldn't have cared less if she ever saw her mother again. Frankie wanted to jump out of her bed, and choke her arrogant, ignorant, shallow, heartless mother at that moment.

"It's good to see that you are awake, darling. You've been sleep for about two months now. How are you feeling?" She placed her hands on Frankie's forehead.

"She was shot Vivian. It's not like she has a fever." Her father always knew what to say. Frankie tried to laugh, but it hurt too much. She placed her hand on her stomach to control her laughing, and at that moment, her heart dropped. She rubbed her stomach again. *Oh hell no.*

Frankie looked down to see a slight bulge in her gown. She looked at Reese with panic written all over her face. Reese inhaled deeply. Frankie looked at her mother. She hadn't wiped the arrogant smirk off her face. Frankie rubbed her stomach again. *Oh hell no! Not again!*

"Am I…" Frankie looked at Reese.

"Yes, hon…you're pregnant." Reese answered, sadly. She knew that Frankie would have a hard time accepting that.

"How far?" Frankie asked as tears filled her eyes, "how far along am I?"

A nurse had walked in as Frankie speaking, and answered the question for her. "Almost five months. You've got some soldiers in there, Mommy." She placed her stethoscope up to Frankie's belly. "They're doing just fine sweetheart. They are miracle babies for sure. We didn't expect them to make it through these last two months."

"They?" Frankie looked puzzled.

"Yes, they. You are having twins." The nurse responded with a huge smile on her face. Little did she know that this was *not* a happy moment for Frankie. This was the worst news that Frankie felt she could have received. *Pregnant? Again? Now I will never get away from him! I'm connected with him for the life of these babies—if he doesn't kill us all first! Dear Lord why did you wake me up? Why didn't you just let me die? Why didn't you let us all just die?*

This was just too much for Frankie to swallow. She closed her eyes in hopes that when she *really* woke up, she would be in her office, approving invoices. Tears streamed down the sides of her face as she drifted back into an unconscious state.

Forty-One

FRANKIE WAS IN and out of consciousness for the next few weeks. Some days, she would wake to the voice of Reese singing to her—which was always a pleasant way to wake up. Some days, she would wake to find Anthony there pacing in front of her bed. She never saw Thomas— which was, on one hand, very relieving. But on the other hand, it was very stressful and scary. She didn't know when she *would* open her eyes to find Thomas standing there, ready to take her home, and finish what he started. One day, she woke up to find her mother standing over her crying. Her mother was wearing no make-up, and had on a casual shirt, and a pair of jeans.

Frankie, reaching up to touch her crying mother's hand, whispered, "Don't cry, Mother."

Vivian opened her eyes. "Hi…Frankie…I'm just talking to God…I haven't done that in a while…" She grabbed Frankie's hand, and sat down in the chair that was next to the bed. Frankie watched. "Frankie, I have to say something to you."

"Yes?"

"Frankie, when you came over that day in tears, and you told me
that he had been hurting you, I didn't want to believe it. I didn't know
what to say. What I said to you was wrong, and I wish that I would have
really listened to you. I am sorry. I know I may seem materialistic and
shallow…and I guess I am…but honestly, I guess I just wanted you to be
just like me. I guess I was jealous at the fact that you didn't *need* a man to
provide for you. Look at you…you've got a great house…a great job
where everyone loves you…you don't need me, your father, or anyone
else. You've got it all. And if Shelton left me today, I would have
nothing. Frankie, I'm proud of you, and I'm so sorry for not being the
mother that I should have been to you." Frankie had been waiting to hear
those words from her mother for years, and when she finally heard them,
she began to cry. Her mother leaned over, and hugged her only child.
They stayed there hugging and crying until Frankie fell asleep in her
mother's arms.

Frankie woke up hours later which felt like days, and the room
was empty. She looked over at all the flowers, cards, and balloons. There
were framed photos that had apparently been taken of her while she was
still in the coma. In one of the photos were all her co-workers,
supervisors, and even Mr. Wallace himself, all huddled around her hospital
bed smiling, and laughing. Another photo featured Reese on one side of
her bed, and June on the other side. June was kissing Frankie on her head.
Then there was one of Reese, Patrice, Yahira, and Sapphire, all with
novelty hats on that had "HAPPY NEW YEARS" printed across the front.
Frankie realized that she had a good life. She had great friends who were
like family. She worked for a very good company. She was awesome at
her job, and she was smart, talented, beautiful, loving, caring, and an

overall good person. Frankie realized there, in that bed, that she was worth so much more. She knew that she didn't need another man to validate her. She was perfect just the way she was. Frankie began to fall in love…with herself. As a tear slid down her left cheek, she drifted back off to sleep, with a smile on her face.

Frankie began to have nightmares about Thomas trying to kill her, and the twins. One particular night, she was having the same nightmare, and instead of being comforted by the voices of the nurses on duty, she was awakened by a man's voice. Startled, she woke up, and began to beg for Thomas to have mercy on her. Anthony's soft voice comforted her instead. She opened her eyes to see Anthony standing over her. She realized that it was only a nightmare. Anthony wiped the sweat from her brow, and kissed her on her head. She smiled, and went back to sleep.

A few more weeks passed, and the doctors felt comfortable allowing Frankie to go home although, it was almost time for her to deliver the babies. She had a set date when they were actually going to perform a Caesarean section. Extreme care had been taken to eliminate any more trauma to the twins.

The doctor finished the discharge paperwork, and the nurses all came in to say their farewells. As they were walking out, Anthony walked in the room. Frankie was trying to slide on her slippers. She was sitting on the edge of the bed, and the slipper kept sliding away from her swollen foot. She was getting frustrated, and began to hyperventilate. Anthony ran over, bent down, and slid the slipper on for her. He patted her other foot, and she lifted it, allowing him to slide the shoe on. Frankie placed her hand on his shoulder, and thanked him. He placed his hand on her large stomach, and kissed her belly. He then stood up, and there they were, face to face. Fear struck Frankie again. She was afraid that Thomas

would walk in, and catch her with Anthony. She pulled back from him.
He looked hurt as fear filled her eyes.

"Who's taking me home, Tony? You?" She looked worried.

"Yes ma'am. At your service." Anthony bowed in front of her.

"Uh…Tony, I don't think that would be a good idea."

"Why not, Key-Lime? Reese is out of town. She asked me to take
you. Your folks ain't in town either." Tony explained. Frankie freaked.

"Oh my God! Oh my God! Oh my God! Don't you guys get it? If
you take me there, and Thomas sees, or finds out, he'll kill me for sure!"
Just then Anthony grabbed Frankie by the hand, and begged her to calm
down. She was breathing uncontrollably, and had begun to sweat. He led
her over to the couch that was near the window—the same couch that had
become his second bed, during the many nights that he prayed over her as
he watched her belly grow. He took a tissue, and wiped her brow.

"I need to tell you something, Frankie. Sit down." Frankie leaned
back, and lowered herself onto the couch. She blew out a deep breath, and
placed her hands on her belly. She looked at Anthony, ready to hear what
he had to say. "Look Frankie…I don't know how to tell you this, but
apparently no one has told you yet…"

"Tony, I really am not in the mood for beatings…let alone *beating*
around the bush. Just tell me."

"Thomas left you for dead."

"Obviously, he shot me!"

"Listen. He left you for dead, and then shot and killed himself."
Frankie's mouth fell open. She didn't know what to feel. Anthony
continued, "But before shooting himself, he poured gasoline around the
house, and set in on fire. Your neighbors heard the commotion, and then
saw him outside. They called the police instantly, and by the time we all

got to the house, it was covered in flames. They pulled you two out, and realized that *you* weren't dead." Tony studied her face. Frankie had turned her head, and was staring off into space. He touched her arm. "Baby, you okay?" He placed his arm around her shoulders. Frankie began to cry. Anthony looked at her, and allowed her to have that moment. He sat there in silence as she cried. She wasn't crying because she was sad that Thomas was dead. She was crying because she was free. She was finally free.

Forty-Two

ANTHONY HELPED FRANKIE climb the steps of the church. He had convinced her to come this particular Sunday, and deep inside, she knew that she really needed to be in church. It had been years since she had attended service. As a child, she would go to church with her parents, but she never had a strong desire to return after she left home for college. Frankie knew that had it not been for God, she *would* have died. She knew that she had no choice *but* to at least attend one service, and give Him thanks.

She waddled up the steps, one at a time, holding onto Anthony's hand. Her stomach was so large, and she could give birth any day now. The church was packed. A warm feeling overtook her as she stepped into the church, and tears began to form. She wanted to really let go and just cry, and she didn't know why.

The ladies at the entrance greeted them, and handed Anthony a pamphlet. He grabbed it, and then followed an usher that led them to vacant seats. Frankie looked around, and observed the members of the church. There were some that were on their knees praying before the

238

service started. There were groups spread throughout the church—groups of men, groups of women, and groups of both. People were greeting each other with hugs and kisses. An older man in a black robe was walking around shaking hands with members of the congregation. Frankie assumed that he was the pastor.

Not too long after that, music began to play softly. Everyone walked to their seats. A man walked out with a microphone in his hands, and began to sing a rendition of Terry Newsome's "Lord, I'm Sorry."

Shedded tears for the years that,
You didn't do right.
Tried to hide your past, your lies, they've cast
Dark shadows over your life.
Time has come and gone still wrong you feel inside
And the pressure it builds
It's time to deal with the real hurt you feel.
God can heal.
I know he will.

Oh, Lord…
I'm sorry for what I've done.
Although, I'm usually not the one
To say
I'm wrong
But if I don't, I can't go on.

The words struck Frankie, and she couldn't hold back the tears. The choir began to sing with the man. Frankie stood up, and raised her hands in the air, and closed her eyes. Then she heard a familiar voice that began adlibbing along with the man. She opened her eyes, and began to cry even more when she saw Reese standing there with a microphone in her hands. She turned to look at Frankie, and sang louder with a huge smile on her face.

Oh, Lord…

Find the good in me

And take out whatever has to be

To let me see

Your heart divine…

I need you in my life.

Frankie was crying uncontrollably at that point, and Reese came down from the platform. She continued to sing to her friend as she cried along with her. Reese removed the microphone from her mouth, and grabbed Frankie. They hugged and cried. The man with the microphone picked up where Reese left off, and continued to sing as others raised their hands to the heavens. Some stood in place, and sang along with the choir. Then some fell down at the altar crying. Frankie asked God to forgive her for choosing to devote her life to a man, and not God himself. Frankie gave her life to the Lord that morning, and vowed that she would never go back to her old life.

Forty-Three

THE WAVES WERE crashing up against the rocks and the sun was shinning bright. The sand felt warm between her toes. The wind was blowing lightly, and there was an occasional mist from the ocean that kissed her face ever so gently. Frankie closed her eyes, and took a deep breath.

She opened her eyes when she felt Reese's hand on hers. She looked over, and smiled. Reese smiled back. Frankie placed her right hand on Reese's large belly, and patted it. Reese grinned, and looked back out into the horizon while placing her left hand over Frankie's. Reese's large diamond ring sparkled in the sunlight.

"You ready?" Frankie asked her glowing friend.

"Yes, girl. I am. You know I am going to miss being pregnant though. It's a beautiful thing. Having a little life growing inside of you…" The wind blew, and both Frankie and Reese leaned their heads back, and inhaled deeply.

"WHO WANTS ICE CREAM?" June yelled as he walked up between the two beach chairs that Frankie and Reese sat in. He was carrying a tray full of ice cream cones.

"YAYYY!!! Ice cream! Ice cream! We want some Uncle Junebug!" The twins hopped up from their sand castles, and ran full force towards June. He braced himself.

"Slow down, girls before you make him drop it." Frankie laughed. The girls stood there holding hands, looking up at June. They reminded Frankie of how she and Reese used to be. June leaned down, and handed the girls their cones.

"One for the lovely little Miss Taylor." He said as he handed the first chocolate cone to the twin on the right.

She replied, "Tank you!" Everyone laughed.

"And one for the lovely little Miss Brooke." June bowed and presented the vanilla cone with sprinkles to the twin on the left. They grabbed their cones, and ran back to their sandcastles screaming with delight.

"Daddy! Daddy! Look what we got!" They stood over Anthony who was buried in the ground under the sand.

"Gimme some!" He teased as he tried to steal a lick from Brooke's cone. She squealed, and ran back to Frankie.

June, Frankie and Reese laughed as they watched the girls devour their cones within a matter of seconds. June leaned down, and kissed his cousin on the head. "How's my favorite cousin feeling?"

"I'm good, Bug." Frankie closed her eyes, and enjoyed the sounds of her daughters laughing and squealing. June turned to Reese, and rubbed her belly as he kissed her on the lips.

"And how is my favorite lady feeling?" He knelt down in the sand on his knees, and kissed her belly. He looked up at her and they kissed again. Frankie just smiled.

The sun was about to set, and it was getting dark. June helped Reese up out of the beach chair. He grabbed her hands, and they started walking back towards the beach house. Reese was waddling right next to him. Frankie smiled at the sight. The girls were whining as Anthony picked them up from their sandcastles. They wanted to stay out later, of course, and didn't want to go to bed. They ran over to Frankie, and grabbed her hands.

"Mommy, what is God? Mrs. Woods was talking about God in Sunday School." Brooke asked as she looked up at her mother. At that moment, Anthony walked up behind her, and placed his hands around Frankie's waist. He picked Taylor up, and kissed Frankie on the cheek. The sun began to set, and Frankie leaned down with Brooke between her arms.

"Girls, you see that?" She said as she pointed to the setting orange sun. The girls nodded. "*That's* God." Frankie stood up, and Anthony put Taylor back on the ground. They stood there as a family, and watched the sun go down behind the waters on the horizon.

As they began to walk back to the beach house, the girls looked up at their mother and in unison said, "Mommy?"

"Yes?" Frankie responded.

"We love you, Mommy!" the little girls sang.

"Love you too…" Frankie responded as she watched her lovely daughters take off running towards the beach house. They had caught up with June and Reese, and were trying to help Reese up the steps. Everyone burst out laughing as the girls placed four little hands on Reese's butt, and began to push her up the steps.

Frankie understood what Ms. Robin was talking about that night. This was the perfect kind of love that she had been searching for, for so long. Frankie finally got it! *She* had to know who *she* was. The things that people would tell her about herself meant nothing if she didn't believe it. She realized that she was worth respect, and love. She learned that she needed to love herself *first* before she could love anyone else. *That's* true happiness. Frankie learned that true happiness did not come from another man, or sex, or even money for that matter. Frankie discovered that true happiness could only come from within. Frankie didn't know how she got there but she knew that she was there.

Desperately Devoted

To purchase your own copy of Terry Newsome's CD entitled Soul Music, and to hear the original version of this very powerful, and soul stirring song "Lord, I'm Sorry," please visit:

http://cdbaby.com/cd/tnewsome2

www.Sonicbids.com/terrynewsome

www.myspace.com/terrynewsomesoulmusic

1-800-BUY-MY-CD

To purchase your own copy of Terry's latest CD entitled Mo Soul Music, please visit:

www.cdbaby.com/tnewsome3

Terry Newsome: This is the name of a ground-breaking, anointed, and dynamic man of God in the gospel music industry. Terry defines his album in the lyrics of the title song "Soul Music"- "music that breaks yokes and inspired by the Holy Ghost."

The album will consist of twenty-one anointed tracks that will bless your soul!

To book Terry Newsome at your next event or to minister at your church, please contact his manager Jennie at 912-492-2002 or email at soulmusicrecords@gmail.com.

K. C. NiBlack

Desperately Devoted

K. C. NiBlack was born in Augusta, GA and spent a lot of her life moving around to various parts of the world as a military brat. Writing has always been a passion of hers, and after realizing one day that she had spent a lot of her life setting goals and never actually accomplishing most of them, she decided to take the first steps to complete a goal that she had set many years ago—writing her first book, Desperately Devoted. K. C. NiBlack also wanted to set an example for her two young daughters, and show them that they could do whatever they set their minds to, regardless of their surroundings and their circumstance. They encouraged her, and cheered her on. As she spent endless hours in front of her laptop punching out her ideas, and pushing through her various surges of writer's block, her daughters both lay at her feet, writing their own stories—which she plans on publishing within the next year. K. C. NiBlack is a woman who has a strong desire to show others how to give their pain, their joys, their desires, and their dreams a voice.

www.ingramcontent.com/pod-product-compliance
Lightning Source LLC
Chambersburg PA
CBHW050506260626
47157CB00004B/1216